ALBERT EINSTEIN

★ ★ ★ ★ ★ ★ ★ ★ ★ ★ ★ ★

Name: Albert Einstein

Born: March 14, 1879

Died: April 18, 1955

Position: Physicist

Career Highlights:

- In 1915, he finished the General Theory of Relativity
- In 1921, he was awarded the Nobel Prize in Physics

Interesting Facts:

- Einstein played both the violin and the piano
- He was asked to be the president of Israel. He declined
- Thanks to his theories, we have television, remote controls, lasers, and DVD players

★ ★ ★ ★ ★ ★ ★ ★ ★ ★ ★ ★

ALBERT EINSTEIN

HISTORY'S ★ ★ALL-STARS

ALBERT EINSTEIN

By **Marie Hammontree**

Illustrated by **Robert Doremus**

ALADDIN

New York London Toronto Sydney New Delhi

This book is a work of fiction. Any references to historical events, real people,
or real places are used fictitiously. Other names, characters, places, and events
are products of the author's imagination, and any resemblance to actual
events or places or persons, living or dead, is entirely coincidental.

ALADDIN

An imprint of Simon & Schuster Children's Publishing Division
1230 Avenue of the Americas, New York, NY 10020
This Aladdin edition December 2014
Copyright © 1961 by the Bobbs-Merrill Company, Inc.
Cover illustration copyright © 2014 by Chris Whetzel
Previously published as Childhood of Famous Americans.
All rights reserved, including the right of reproduction in whole or in part in any form.
ALADDIN is a trademark of Simon & Schuster, Inc., and related logo is a registered
trademark of Simon & Schuster, Inc.
For information about special discounts for bulk purchases, please contact Simon &
Schuster Special Sales at 1-866-506-1949 or business@simonandschuster.com.
Cover designed by Laura Lyn DiSiena
Interior designed by Mike Rosamilia
The text of this book was set in Adobe Caslon Pro.
Manufactured in the United States of America 1114 OFF
2 4 6 8 10 9 7 5 3 1
Library of Congress Catalog Card Number 2014933323
ISBN 978-1-4814-1497-5 (hardcover)
ISBN 978-1-4814-1496-8 (paperback)
ISBN 978-1-4814-1498-2 (eBook)

To
Edith Haynel Brand

★ ILLUSTRATIONS ★

Full Pages

Numerous smaller illustrations

★ CONTENTS ★

BOOKS BY MARIE HAMMONTREE

Albert Einstein: Young Thinker

A. P. Giannini: Boy of San Francisco

Will and Charlie Mayo: Boy Doctors

THE COMPASS

ONE DAY IN 1884 Mr. Hermann Einstein came home from work carrying a small package. It was a present for his five-year-old son, Albert, who was in bed with a cold.

"I thought Albert would enjoy this compass," he said to his wife. "He's such a serious boy."

"A compass!" Mrs. Einstein took the strange-looking present and examined it closely. It was a tiny round box with a glass lid. Under the glass, a needle swung on a pivot or pin in the center of the box. One half of the needle was colored dark. The bottom of the box bore the words *North, East, South,* and *West.*

"Now watch the compass work," said her husband. Slowly he turned the compass in one direction, then in another. "See how the needle spins around? No matter which way the box is turned, the dark end of the needle will point to the north."

It did indeed! Mrs. Einstein watched with interest as her husband turned the compass.

Now Mr. Einstein continued. "All you have to do is move the compass so that the word *North* is under the dark end of the needle. Then you can tell the other directions easily."

Mrs. Einstein was delighted. "Albert loves puzzles," she said, "and that's a puzzle if I ever saw one."

"Then this compass should keep him busy for hours," said Mr. Einstein.

Mrs. Einstein laughed. "You're going to be a busy man, Hermann. Have you forgotten all the questions that Albert will ask?"

Mr. Einstein pretended to groan. How well he remembered! Most of the time Albert was so quiet that people hardly knew he was about. When he was puzzled about something, however, there was no end to the questions he could ask.

Then Mr. Einstein began to laugh. "It will be a good joke on me, Pauline. I suppose I might as well take the compass in to Albert now and face his questions."

"Yes, Hermann, and I'm going with you. I just know Albert is going to be a great professor someday. I would like to hear what he thinks of this compass."

The Einsteins were a Jewish family who lived in Munich, Germany. There were four persons in the family—Mr. and Mrs. Einstein, Albert, and his three-year-old sister Maja. Mr. Einstein's brother Jacob lived with them, too. There was also a fat green parrot named Laura, who thought she was boss of the Einstein home.

Laura talked all the time. Sometimes Mr. and Mrs. Einstein said she was a nuisance, but Albert loved her. Laura was talking now as Mr. and Mrs. Einstein approached Albert's room.

"Somebody's coming! Somebody's coming!" she said in a loud voice.

"Oh, Laura, it's only Father and Mother," Albert said with a smile.

"Your father has a present for you, Albert," Mrs. Einstein said. "A compass!"

"What's a compass?" asked Albert.

"What's a compass?" repeated Laura.

Mr. Einstein turned to the parrot. "Quiet, Laura. Let Albert enjoy his present."

"Quiet, Laura!" the parrot repeated loudly. "Laura's a bad girl. Tsk, tsk, tsk! Take her out of the room."

"That's a splendid idea." Mrs. Einstein picked up Laura's cage and started for the door.

"Poor Laura!" Albert laughed.

"Noisy Laura," said Mr. Einstein.

"Bad bird!" Laura wailed. "Bad bird!"

When Mrs. Einstein returned to the room, father and son were bending over the compass. Albert's questions had already begun.

"What's a compass for? How can a needle in a box tell which way is north? Why does the needle turn around?"

"Questions, questions, questions!" Mr. Einstein shook his head laughingly. "Maybe if I tell a story, it will help you to understand how a compass works."

Albert's brown eyes lighted up with joy. There was nothing that he loved better than a story. "Yes, Father, please do." He snuggled back in his pillows and waited for the story to begin.

Mrs. Einstein pulled up a chair and sat down.

"Well," Mr. Einstein began, "once an old woodsman named Hans lived deep in a forest not far from Munich."

"Was he very old?" asked Albert.

"Very old," his father repeated, "but even though he was very old, he never had learned how to find his way in the forest."

"My goodness!" cried Mrs. Einstein. "A woodsman who couldn't find his way in the forest would certainly be in a fix."

Mr. Einstein nodded. "Poor old Hans was in a fix all right. He had been lost more times than Albert can count."

"I can count to a hundred," Albert said.

"I know you can, son, and Hans had been lost more than a hundred times. Each morning when he left the house, Mrs. Hans would worry and worry. Sometimes it would be days before Hans could find his way home. His wife would think, 'Oh, my, this time my Hans has surely been eaten up by a bear.'"

"Of course, she would," agreed Mrs. Einstein.

"I'm glad you're not a woodsman, Hermann, or I should worry, too."

"Aha, but I wouldn't get lost!" Mr. Einstein said. "I'd have a compass to tell me the direction I needed to go."

"So that's what a compass is for!" Albert exclaimed. "To keep you from getting lost!"

"Right!" said his father. "It's exactly what Mrs. Hans decided to get for old Hans. One day she came into Munich and bought the best compass she could find. She wasn't going to have Hans getting lost anymore. Then what do you think Hans did?"

"He asked how the compass worked," laughed Mrs. Einstein, "just as Albert did."

Albert giggled. His mother was teasing, of course. She and his father often teased him about his questions, but they always did their best to answer them.

"Well, Father," Albert said, "how *did* the compass work?"

"Hans thought ghosts were making it work," his father said. "He said spirits swung that needle back to the north when he turned the compass around."

Albert and his mother laughed. What a foolish fellow Hans was! Everybody knew there were no such things as ghosts.

"Mrs. Hans knew better, however," Mr. Einstein went on. "She had asked the storekeeper to tell her about the compass when she bought it, and this is what he said."

Albert sat up in bed and Mrs. Einstein pulled her chair closer. They wanted to hear what the storekeeper had said.

"A compass needle is really a magnet," Mr. Einstein said.

"Of course!" Albert said, nodding his head.

"I've seen a magnet. Mother uses one to pick up needles from the floor when she sews."

"That's right, son," said Mr. Einstein. "Now every magnet has two ends. One end is called 'north' and the other 'south.' If you put the north ends of two magnets together, they will fly apart. Two south ends will do the same thing."

"What about a north end and a south end?" asked Albert curiously.

"That's the strange thing," replied his father. "A north end and a south end attract each other."

"What does that have to do with a compass?" Mrs. Einstein wanted to know.

"Well, my dear, this is the part that is hard to believe. It's the part that old Hans couldn't believe at all. The earth itself is a big magnet. Any small magnet, when it isn't fastened, will begin to turn. It will turn until the south end of the magnet is pointing north."

"My goodness!" cried Mrs. Einstein. "It makes one feel odd to think that we're living on a big magnet, doesn't it?"

Mr. Einstein and Albert both laughed. Still, they agreed that the idea did make them feel a little strange.

"Go on," said Albert. "Tell us more about Hans. Did he ever learn to use the compass?"

"Yes, finally, but not until he had had a very bad fright. One day he was out chopping wood. Suddenly a big bear came up to him, just as Mrs. Hans had always feared."

"Did the bear chase him?"

"It certainly did. Old Hans ran and ran. Finally he lost the bear."

"By that time I'll bet Hans was really lost, too," said Mrs. Einstein.

"He was," said Mr. Einstein. "At last when he found his way home, he was a mighty tired and hungry man. He decided that even if spirits did make the compass needle turn, he'd rather trust the compass than get lost again."

"So this time he listened to Mrs. Hans?" Mrs. Einstein asked.

"Yes, indeed. She showed him how to use the compass, and he never got lost again."

"Oh, my goodness!" Mrs. Einstein jumped from her chair. "Your story was so interesting that I almost forgot our supper! I hope it hasn't burned up."

Fortunately, supper wasn't burned. Mrs. Einstein brought Albert's supper to him on a tray. She had cooked chicken and dumplings, one of Albert's favorite dishes. She had also made a big cherry tart.

After supper, Albert looked at his compass.

"It certainly is strange about the earth being a magnet," he thought. "I wonder what makes it a magnet? Father didn't explain that."

He turned the compass around in his hands and watched the needle swing always to the north. "Father didn't explain how the magnet became a magnet, either," he thought. "I guess I'll have to ask him."

COUSINS FROM THE BLACK FOREST

COMPANY HAD COME last night, and Albert was delighted. His uncle, aunt, and three cousins had come from the Black Forest to pay a visit. The Black Forest was west of Munich.

Uncle Rudolph was Albert's father's brother and Uncle Rudolph's wife was Albert's mother's sister. Accordingly their three daughters, Hermine, Elsa, and Paula, and Albert and Maja were double cousins.

Albert liked his cousins. They were friendly and kind and never made him feel bashful.

When some people came to visit, Albert wanted to run away and hide, but not when his cousins came.

Albert wouldn't have wanted to hide today, anyway. This was the first day of the *Oktoberfest*, which was held each fell in Munich. The festival was to start at noon, and right now all the Einsteins were getting ready to go.

"Hurry," Uncle Rudolph called to the others. "We don't want to miss the parade."

"I'm ready," said Mr. Einstein, coming from his room. He was dressed for the holiday in a Bavarian peasant costume. He wore short leather pants, red suspenders, long socks, and a little hat with a cocky feather. Uncle Rudolph was wearing the same kind of costume.

Then the two mothers entered the room. They were wearing peasant costumes, too, and they looked as pretty as could be. Both wore white blouses and black bodices laced across the front. Lively hats matched their green and yellow skirts.

"We're ready," they said together.

"So are we," cried the girls. All four were wearing their best Sunday dresses and looked just as pretty as their mothers.

"Me, too!" Albert said. He was just as neat as the girls.

Laura, the parrot, was sitting on her perch in the corner of the room. In the excitement she had been forgotten, even by Albert. "Me, too," she croaked. "Me, too!"

Everyone laughed.

"No," Uncle Rudolph said, "parrots can't go."

Then the Einsteins left the house and went to the corner to wait for a streetcar. When the car came, pulled by a trotting horse, the Einsteins got on quickly. The car was already crowded

with people headed for the big meadow where the *Oktoberfest* was to be held. Everyone was talking and laughing at once. Albert sat watching and listening happily.

On the way to the meadow Albert suddenly said, "Father, why do we have the *Oktoberfest?*"

"Well, it started a long time ago, in 1810," Mr. Einstein said. "The son of the King of Bavaria was going to be married. The King thought it would be nice to give the people of Bavaria a present. He gave a big wedding feast, and everybody was welcome to come."

"Everybody had so much fun that the people of Munich didn't want to give up the festival," Uncle Rudolph went on. "Now for two weeks each fall they celebrate again."

"The first thing you will see in the parade is a statue of a little monk with outstretched arms," said Mrs. Einstein.

"Oh, I know who he is!" Hermine cried. "He's the child of Munich."

"Yes, indeed," Mrs. Einstein went on. "He's the symbol of our city. You know, Munich was first settled by Catholic monks many hundreds of years ago."

Presently the streetcar reached the meadow where the festival was to be held. A great crowd was gathered there. Everybody was dressed in bright clothes. The men wore leather shorts like Mr. Einstein's and Uncle Rudolph's. The women wore peasant costumes like Mrs. Einstein's. The boys and girls were dressed gaily, too, just as Albert and his sister and cousins were.

"Look!" Maja called. "Here comes the parade."

"This is a good place to watch it," said Mr. Einstein. "Let's get off right here."

When the streetcar stopped, he jumped off

and the rest of the Einsteins followed him. They lined up along the street to watch the parade as it turned into the meadow.

What a parade it was! It was just as good as a circus parade. Uncle Rudolph said it was the best parade he had ever seen. Albert thought so, too. His eyes grew wide as he watched the brass bands march by and saw the flower-covered carts drawn by handsome big horses.

At last the parade ended.

"My goodness, I'm hungry!" Mr. Einstein exclaimed. "Let's have something to eat."

Everybody agreed that this was a fine idea. Led by Mr. Einstein, the family strolled through the meadow.

"Oh, dear!" said Mrs. Einstein. "What if we can't make up our minds what we want?"

"I know what I want," Hermine said. "I'd like some sausages and buns."

"That ox roasting over the charcoal fire looks good to me," said Elsa.

"How about roast chicken?" asked Uncle Rudolph eagerly.

"No, no!" said his wife. "I want one of those wonderful onion pies with apple cider."

"Don't forget, Father," Maja cried. "You promised I could have plum cake."

Mr. Einstein laughed. "You'll get your plum cake, Maja. Everybody is going to choose exactly what he wants to eat. This is a holiday, and we'll all do as we wish."

"After that we'll visit the shows and join in the dancing," Uncle Rudolph added.

When they had finished eating, Uncle Rudolph took the family to one of the shows. First they saw a tattooed man, then a fat woman who needed three chairs to sit on, then a huge snake. Albert liked the show, especially the snake.

Next Uncle Rudolph led the family across the meadow to a place where people were dancing. On the way, he passed a man selling balloons.

"See the balloons, children!" he said. "Would you like one?"

"Oh, yes, Father!" cried Hermine. "Please get us a balloon."

Uncle Rudolph dug down in the pocket of his leather shorts and took out some money, which he gave to the man. "All right," he said. "Each of you may pick the balloon you want."

Maja chose a green balloon, Albert a blue one, Elsa a red one, and Paula a yellow one. Hermine chose a white balloon with a picture of the little monk of Munich on it. Each balloon had a long string tied to it.

"Now then!" Uncle Rudolph said. "Let's go dancing." He took his wife by the hand, and together they walked through the crowds to an open space where people were dancing. Mr. and Mrs. Einstein followed quickly.

Albert and the girls sat down along the side of the dancing area to watch. The girls' eyes shone with eagerness, but not Albert's. Albert thought dancing was foolish. His eyes kept turning up to look at his balloon.

"You're not going to dance, are you, Albert?" Hermine said after a while.

Albert shook his head.

"Then would you mind holding our balloons for us while we dance?"

"Of course not," Albert said. "Go right ahead and dance if you want to. I'll just sit here and hold the balloons and watch."

Each of the girls gave Albert her balloon and joined the dancers. Now he had five balloons.

After a while he noticed that one of the strings had become tangled. "I guess I might as well get it loose," he thought. "This silly dancing isn't any fun to watch."

He began to untangle the string. Suddenly it came loose. Without warning the balloon rose swiftly into the air.

"Oh, dear!" Albert tried to catch the string. "That was Maja's balloon. Well, I'll give her mine. It's just as pretty."

He settled back to watch the balloon soar upward, over the heads of the dancers. "I wonder where it's going?" he thought as it moved higher and farther away. "I wonder why it went up instead of sidewards or down?"

Soon the balloon disappeared in the distance. Albert looked at the remaining balloons. "Maybe there was something different about Maja's," he thought. "I think I'll set another one free to find out."

This time he chose Elsa's red balloon. It was

not a bit different from the green one. It rose up and up in the sky. Albert watched it happily until it was out of sight. This was a lot more fun than watching the dancers!

Albert eyed the remaining balloons. His eyes were thoughtful. "I wonder—"

Up went the blue balloon, rising and drifting until it disappeared. Then the yellow balloon sailed away and only Hermine's white balloon remained. Should he let it go, too?

Albert looked at the picture of the little monk of Munich. How funny and fat he looked on the side of the balloon! Hermine wouldn't want to lose him.

Still, Albert couldn't help wondering whether this balloon would rise like the others.

"I wonder what's up there in the sky?" he thought. "It would be fun to sail off in Hermine's balloon and find out."

Almost by itself, the string of Hermine's balloon seemed to leave Albert's fingers, and the balloon drifted upward. At that moment the music stopped and the dancers paused to rest. Albert didn't notice. He was watching the balloon.

Suddenly the girls cried out.

"Albert!"

"Our balloons!"

"Where are they?"

The girls took one look in the direction in which Albert was staring, and knew. Albert had been having fun, too, but not with dancing.

"Oh, Albert!" Elsa exclaimed sadly. "Our beautiful new balloons!"

Albert dropped his head. He was sorry now. He hadn't kept his promise, and it was wrong not to keep a promise. If only he had some money, he would buy more balloons. He didn't have any, though, and had no way to get any.

He looked so unhappy that Elsa could bear it no longer. "Never mind, Albert," she told him. "After all, you don't care for dancing. You have a right to enjoy yourself, too."

"Yes, I suppose so," Hermine agreed. "Still, I had such a pretty balloon!"

"We can get another one," her father said.

Albert lifted his head. He felt better now that nobody was angry.

When the Einsteins went home from the festival that night, they were all tired but happy. There would be two more weeks of merrymaking during the *Oktoberfest,* and the Einsteins would probably go again.

For Albert, however, there could hardly be a better day than today. He had found another puzzle to think about. What lay beyond this big earth magnet? Where had those balloons gone? Would they ever come down to earth again?

IS ALBERT STUBBORN?

ONE DAY ALBERT was practicing on his violin. He was nine years old now and had been taking violin lessons for some time. He did not play well at all.

"Albert, you don't play well because you don't practice," his mother told him. "Today you must promise to practice for a whole hour."

"Yes, Mother," Albert agreed. "I will."

He went into the living room and opened his violin case. He would do his very best today. He really wanted to please his mother.

"If only I could play something besides scales I would like to practice better," he said aloud.

"I heard that, Albert," his mother said from the other room. "There's only one way to learn and that is to do a thing over and over."

"Yes, Mother," Albert said. He lifted the violin to his chin and began.

"C, D, E, F, G, A, B, C."

When he reached the end of the scale, Albert stopped. That was a good place to stop and rest. He looked out the window. A stork was moving around in its big shapeless nest on the roof. "I wish I could see what that old stork is doing," Albert thought.

"Albert!"

"Yes, Mother."

"C, B, A, G, F, E, D, C."

This time Albert played six scales before he laid his violin down.

30

"Mother!"

"What is it, Albert?"

Mrs. Einstein came into the living room. She carried her sewing, and she chose a nice easy chair. She might as well sit down. Otherwise Albert would soon be out in the garden, and the practicing wouldn't be done.

"It always sounds so pretty when you play the piano. Why can't I play as well as you?"

"You can, Albert. Already you play a few simple pieces. You could do much better if you would practice more."

"I get so tired," he said. "I don't like to play the same thing over and over again."

"That's the way I learned to play the piano. I used to practice for hours when I was a little girl. It's the only way you can learn."

"All right." Albert sighed as he picked up his violin. "I'll practice."

Mrs. Einstein sighed, too. Other children could repeat their lessons a few times and have them learned, but not Albert. Albert was a good boy and he obeyed his parents, but he didn't like to study. At least, he didn't like to study in the same way other children did.

"Maybe you would like me to accompany you on the piano?" Mrs. Einstein asked. "How about the 'Cradle Song' by Brahms?"

"Oh, yes! I'll get my music," Albert replied.

Albert really tried, but even his mother's fine playing couldn't cover up the squeaky sounds of his violin. By the end of an hour he began to improve, but he had to admit that the "Cradle Song" needed a great deal of practice.

Suddenly Mrs. Einstein had an idea. "Albert, what is your favorite subject in school?"

"Why, you know, Mother," he said in surprise. "It's mathematics."

"Well, then, have you ever thought how much mathematics there is in music?"

Albert smiled. "Oh, Mother, you're teasing! Who ever heard of mathematics in music?"

"No, Albert, I'm not teasing at all," she went on. "Think about it for a moment. When you play a piece of music, don't you count time?"

"Why—why, of course I do!" Albert exclaimed in surprise. "I hadn't thought about that before. It isn't always the same time, either. For a march you count one, two, three, four—one, two, three, four."

"How do you count for a waltz?"

Albert thought for a while, then smiled. "One, two, three—one, two, three."

"Good!" his mother said. "Now you're beginning to understand."

Still smiling with pleasure over learning something new, Albert picked up his violin. "I guess I *will* practice some more."

Mrs. Einstein left the room. She was happy. At last she had succeeded in making Albert interested in practicing. She told her husband about it as soon as he came home from his electrical shop that night.

"Well, well!" he exclaimed with pleasure. "Now if we could only find a way to get Albert interested in school."

"Hermann, I think our German schools are too strict," Mrs. Einstein said.

"That's true." Mr. Einstein nodded. "Children are treated as if they were soldiers."

"Albert tells me he must stand at attention whenever he's called upon to recite," Mrs. Einstein went on.

"Some teachers even whip a pupil if he speaks without being spoken to," Mr. Einstein added.

"Albert is too gentle for such treatment."

"He's stubborn, Pauline."

Mrs. Einstein shook her head. "I wouldn't call him stubborn, Hermann. He just doesn't like to be ordered around."

"I don't know, Pauline," Mr. Einstein said a little doubtfully. "His teachers say Albert is dull. His grades are the lowest in the class."

"No, no, Hermann," Mrs. Einstein objected. "He does very well in mathematics."

"Yes, but there are other subjects besides mathematics. Albert has to learn those subjects, too," Mr. Einstein reminded her.

Mrs. Einstein sighed. What her husband said was true. She knew Albert, however. Nobody could force him against his will. If anyone tried, he would soon find that it was no use.

"HONEST JOHN"

A few days later Albert's classmates were playing in the schoolyard during recess.

"Let's play soldier," said one of the boys, whose name was Frederick. "Come on, Albert. Do you want to play with us?"

Albert smiled and shook his head. "No, thank you," he said. "I'll just sit here and watch." He went over to the steps of the school and sat down. He seldom played with the other children, and never wanted to play soldier.

"All right then. The rest of us will play," Frederick said. "I'll be general today. Fall in, everybody! Fall in!"

The other boys lined up.

"Atten-*tion*!"

The boys drew themselves as stiff as ramrods.

"Forward, march!"

The boys marched around the yard, kicking their legs out stiffly in the goosestep that German soldiers used.

"One, two, three, four!" Frederick shouted as

he marched at the head of the column. "Left, right! Left, right!"

At that moment a company of real soldiers came marching past the school. At the head of the company was an officer, riding on a horse.

When the boys saw the soldiers, they marched more stiffly and proudly than ever.

"One, two, three, four!" Frederick shouted loudly. "To the rear, march!"

Each boy turned in his tracks, and the column marched in the opposite direction, away from the street, with Frederick in the lead. Suddenly a loud voice behind them shouted, "Halt!"

Startled, the boys stopped where they were. This wasn't Frederick shouting. It was a man! The boys turned around. It was the officer, who had halted his company and ridden his horse over to the edge of the schoolyard.

The boys were frightened. Some were even

too frightened to move. An army officer was an important person in Germany in those days.

"Good work, boys," the officer said. "You will make fine soldiers someday."

Frederick and the others straightened their shoulders proudly.

"Thank you, sir," Frederick said. "We would like to be good soldiers."

He and his friends went over to talk to the soldiers. They admired the soldiers' shiny black boots and the brass buttons on their uniforms.

Meanwhile, Albert sat on the steps, thinking and dreaming. He didn't even notice that the soldiers had stopped.

"Who's that boy?" asked the officer, pointing to Albert.

"Oh, that's 'Honest John,'" Frederick said with a laugh. He felt quite bold now.

"'Honest John?' Why do you call him that?"

"Because he's not very bright," said another boy, named Wilhelm. "He always tells the truth, even if it gets him in trouble."

The soldiers laughed, and so did the boys.

"Call him over here," said the officer. "I want to talk with this 'Honest John.'"

Frederick hurried over to get Albert. Albert came, but he came unwillingly. He wasn't interested in soldiers.

"Yes, sir?" he said.

"What's your name?" asked the officer.

"Albert Einstein."

"The boys tell me it's 'Honest John.'"

"They call me that sometimes, sir."

"They're making fun of you. Don't you care?"

"It doesn't matter," said Albert. "I don't think they mean any harm."

The soldiers laughed again.

"Why aren't you playing soldiers with the

rest of the boys?" the officer went on. "Won't they let you play with them?"

"Oh, yes, they asked me to play, but I didn't want to," Albert answered. "I'm not going to be a soldier."

The officer's face grew stern. "Every German boy becomes a soldier when he grows up!"

"I'm not going to be one," Albert said with feeling. "Never!"

The boys were frightened. They hadn't

expected this. What would the officer do? They didn't want to see poor Albert shot.

"What impudence!" exclaimed the officer. "Where do you live?"

By this time Albert was frightened, too—so frightened that he was shaking all over. He wanted to run, but he didn't. In a low voice he told the officer where he lived.

Albert's schoolmates watched and listened with growing respect. Albert might be an "Honest John" who didn't know any better than to tell the truth, but he certainly wasn't a coward!

Suddenly a teacher came to the door of the building and rang a bell. Recess was over. It was one recess when the teacher didn't have to ring twice. Not one boy hung back in the schoolyard today!

Albert was still frightened when he got

home that evening. He told his mother and father what had happened. They were frightened, too.

"I don't want to be a soldier, Father!" Albert cried. "That officer was ordering those poor soldiers to march here and there just as if—as if they were animals. He'd ordered them to kill people, too, and I won't do it!"

"Every German boy has to serve in the army when he grows up," Mr. Einstein said.

"I won't," Albert declared. "I don't want to be a German. Father, please take me away."

Mr. Einstein put his arm around the boy's shoulders. "It's still a long time before you'll be old enough to go in the army, Albert. Let's not worry about that yet."

Albert did worry, however. For weeks he shivered and shook whenever he heard a knock at the door. What if it was the officer?

However, the officer never came. Maybe he admired Albert's courage. Maybe he thought Albert would not make a good soldier. Maybe he had forgotten Albert's address. Albert hoped the last was true.

NO SCHOOL TODAY

SEVERAL WEEKS HAD passed. Albert no longer had nightmares about the officer. In fact, he slept so soundly that one morning he didn't even hear his mother call him. He heard Laura, though. A person would have to be deaf not to hear Laura.

"Time to get up!" the parrot repeated after Mrs. Einstein. "Time to get up!"

"Oh, Laura!" Albert turned over. His bed was covered with a large quilt filled with goose feathers. The quilt was as light as a cream puff and as warm as toast. It felt so good that Albert hated to leave the bed.

He closed his eyes again. He would pretend that he was still asleep. Laura wouldn't know.

Then he remembered that today was a holiday, and he jumped out of bed in a hurry. How could he have forgotten that there was no school today? How could he have forgotten that his father and Uncle Jacob had promised he could visit their shop today?

Hermann and Jacob Einstein owned an electrical shop, where they made electric batteries. The shop was right next door to the Einstein home, but Albert was seldom permitted to play in it. When he was, however, Albert was the happiest boy in town.

Albert had his clothes on in a moment. In another moment he was dashing into the kitchen.

"My, my!" Uncle Jacob said. "What a hurry you're in this morning!"

Albert grinned. He knew what Uncle Jacob meant. So did the rest of the family. Albert was as slow as cold molasses on mornings when he had to go to school.

The Einsteins sat down to breakfast. It was a hearty breakfast, too. Nobody could cook sausages like Mrs. Einstein. Her coffee cake was delicious. Albert ate hungrily.

After breakfast Mrs. Einstein handed Albert a package. "Here's a gingerbread man in case you get hungry after a while," she said.

"Thank you, Mother."

"Now, Albert, remember to keep out of the way," Mrs. Einstein added as Albert left the house with his uncle and father.

"I will," Albert called back happily.

"What a fine day it is!" said Mr. Einstein,

looking up at the blue sky before they entered the shop. "Just imagine today what a wonderful view there will be of the Alps."

"Too nice a day for a boy to play inside," said Uncle Jacob.

Albert shook his head vigorously. Nice day or not, he would rather poke his nose in some dark corner of the Einstein electrical shop.

There were several helpers in the shop. They were already at work when the Einsteins walked in. "Good morning, young fellow," they said. They were always glad to see Albert. He never bothered them or got in their way.

"Good morning," said Albert. He climbed up on a pile of boxes and made himself comfortable. He liked nothing better than to sit there and watch the men at their work.

"He's one of the strangest boys I've ever seen," said one of the helpers, named Karl.

"My boy couldn't wait to go hiking today," said another.

"Well, I'll say this much for Albert," another of the workmen said. "He knows enough to keep out from under our feet."

"That's true," Karl agreed. "Playing around electricity is dangerous business. Some boys would bother us so we couldn't work."

Albert didn't know the men were talking about him, but he wouldn't have cared if he had known. Electricity puzzled him, just as the compass had. As he sat there on the boxes, he was busy trying to figure it out.

Uncle Jacob was an electrical engineer. Albert had asked him a thousand questions about electricity. He wanted to know what it was and how it worked.

"There are many things we don't know about electricity," Uncle Jacob had told him one day.

"However, we do know that it is a kind of force or current that can be used to make light or to to make things run.

"The batteries we make in our shop are filled with chemicals that generate or create this electric current," he went on. "When a person wants to put a battery to work, he connects a wire from one side of the battery to the light. Then he connects a wire from the light to the other side of the battery.

"As soon as this is done, the light burns. We don't know just what happens, but we do know the current flows from one side of the battery through the light to the other side."

As Albert sat on the pile of boxes this morning, he was thinking about this strange current.

"Albert," Uncle Jacob called suddenly, "what about that gingerbread man?"

Albert jumped. He had been thinking so hard that he had forgotten where he was.

The men laughed. So did Albert.

"I'll bet you were asleep," one man teased.

"No, I wasn't," Albert said. "I was thinking."

"That's true," said Uncle Jacob. "The boy's a thinker. Every now and then I catch him lost in thought." He winked at Albert. "I believe 'absent-minded' is the word people use."

There was a shout of laughter at this. Albert laughed, too. He liked nothing better than a joke, even a joke on himself.

WHAT IS ALGEBRA?

Presently Mr. Einstein called Albert into the office. He was the business man of the Einstein shop. He thought Albert might like to see his work. Albert went, but he knew he wouldn't find his father's desk interesting. It never was.

Uncle Jacob's desk was different. Today it was covered with papers. From one end to the other the papers were covered with letters and marks. Albert looked at them in surprise. They didn't mean a thing.

"Uncle Jacob, what are you doing?" Albert asked when Uncle Jacob entered the office.

"I'm working a problem by algebra."

"What's algebra?"

"Well," said Uncle Jacob with a smile, "algebra is a lazy kind of arithmetic. When you don't know what something is, you call it x. Then you start to look for it. Along the way you may meet other things that you don't know, so you give them names, too."

"Like y or z?"

"Right! Then you keep on adding, multiplying, dividing, and subtracting."

"Do you ever find out what they are?"

"Of course you do. Would you like to try it sometime, Albert?"

"Oh, yes! Now?"

Uncle Jacob shook his head. "I'm sorry, but I have to finish this problem of my own now."

Albert was disappointed, but he said nothing. Uncle Jacob was a busy man. It was better to let him finish his work. The sooner it was finished, the sooner he would have time to show Albert what algebra was.

Albert went quietly back to the shop. Again he climbed up on the boxes in the corner. He thought about algebra for a long time. At last his brown eyes closed. His dark head nodded. This time he was really asleep.

He didn't hear the men when they finished their work and left the shop.

He didn't hear his father say, "I have some business calls to make, Jacob. Don't forget to wake up Albert when you're ready to leave."

He didn't hear Uncle Jacob answer, "Yes, yes," or see him return to his problem. Neither did he hear Uncle Jacob when he turned off the light and went out, locking the door of the shop behind him.

Albert was alone in the electrical shop, but he didn't know it. He was still sound asleep.

When Uncle Jacob walked through the garden and into the house without Albert, Mrs. Einstein cried, "Jacob! Where's Albert?"

Uncle Jacob stared at her in astonishment.

"Oh, my goodness!" he exclaimed, and rushed back to the shop.

The Einsteins had great fun teasing Uncle Jacob that evening. Albert had the most fun of all. First he winked at Uncle Jacob. Then he said, "I think Uncle Jacob is absent-minded."

There wasn't a thing Uncle Jacob could say to that except, "Come on, Albert, let me show you how to work an algebra problem."

TROUBLE FOR
THE EINSTEINS

ONE DAY MAJA came home from school with a cat in her arms. "Poor kitty!" she said. "She's wet and hungry. I don't think she has any home, Mother."

"We'll give her a home," said Mrs. Einstein. She wrapped a towel around the shivering cat and rubbed her gently.

"She ought to have a name," said Albert.

Maja agreed. "I'll call her Gertrude. That's the name of my best friend at school."

"Gertrude's a pretty name," said Albert. "I think she's a pretty cat."

"Indeed she is!" said their mother. "She looks as if she's wearing a little black coat with four white mittens."

"Look at the fur under her chin," said Maja proudly. "She's wearing a white bib, too."

Mr. Einstein and Uncle Jacob both liked Gertrude. Indeed, the only member of the family that didn't like the newcomer was Laura.

Gertrude was a smart cat and soon learned her name. Laura learned it, too.

"Gertrude! Gertrude!" she would call, just as Maja did.

At first Gertrude came running when Laura called. Then one day when she ran to the parrot's cage, Laura pecked her on the nose. Gertrude hissed and Laura hissed back.

"Oh! Oh!" said Mrs. Einstein. "What are we going to do?"

"Maybe they're like the ends of a magnet." Albert laughed. "They're both north or both south. That's why they don't get along."

Maja held Gertrude close and smoothed her ruffled fur. "It isn't funny, Albert," she said. "Laura pecked Gertrude on the nose."

"I'm sorry about that," replied Albert, "but why was Gertrude so close to Laura's cage?"

"Laura called her!" Maja answered. "Don't you come when you're called?"

"Children! Children!" said Mrs. Einstein.

Maja took her pet to the kitchen for a bowl of milk. Albert brought some nuts for Laura. He hoped she would forget about the cat while cracking the nuts with her big curved bill.

GERTRUDE HAS A FEAST

The next day was March 14, 1889, Albert's tenth birthday. Whether it was his birthday or not, he had to go to school.

"When you come home, there will be some presents for you," his father told him.

"Yes, and we'll have all your favorite dishes for supper, as we always do on birthdays," his mother said.

Then she set to work to keep her promise. She built a roaring fire in her big stove. She baked bread. She kneaded dough and wrapped it around cherries and bits of apples and peaches. The kitchen had never smelled so good.

When the fish peddler came by, she bought the biggest pike he had. Then she cleaned it and stuffed it with mushrooms, onions, and peppers. Albert liked baked pike.

Next she placed her whitest tablecloth on

the table, then her best silver and her prettiest dishes. At last everything was ready. The children returned from school. Mr. Einstein and Uncle Jacob came home from work.

"Let's go into the sitting room first," said Mr. Einstein. "Albert can open his presents."

"I hope I get some books," said Albert.

He wasn't disappointed. His father and Uncle Jacob had both given him books. Maja gave him a beautiful top carved in the Black Forest. Mrs. Einstein had knitted a muffler to keep him warm during the cold winters.

"Now let's eat!" Uncle Jacob said, sniffing the air eagerly.

The family sat down at the dining room table while Mrs. Einstein went to the kitchen to bring in the fish. She had left it on the table ready to serve.

Suddenly the others heard her cry out. "Oh, my fish! My fish! *Gertrude!*"

The family rushed to the kitchen. The fish lay under the table, not on it, and Gertrude was having the feast of her life!

"It's my fault," said Mrs. Einstein sorrowfully. "I should have put the fish where Gertrude couldn't get it. I should have remembered that cats like fish."

"No, it's my fault, Mother," Maja sobbed. "It was Gertrude who spoiled Albert's dinner, and she's my cat."

"Don't cry, Maja," Albert said. "Sometimes Laura is bad, too. Remember the time I let her out of her cage and forgot to watch her?"

"I remember," said his father. "She chewed the legs of your mother's lovely piano. The marks will always be there."

"Come, dear, dry your eyes," said Mrs. Einstein. "I can always get another fish."

Hopefully Maja turned to Albert. "Then you won't blame Gertrude?"

"Of course not," he said, trying to smile.

After supper Uncle Jacob told Albert that a neighbor had seen Gertrude. She thought Gertrude looked exactly like the missing cat of a friend of hers. She had promised to tell the friend about Gertrude. That made Albert feel much happier about the cat.

POOR LAURA

The next day Albert was in his father's study, reading one of his new books. Mrs. Einstein, who liked flowers, was out in the garden with Maja, planning what she would plant for the coming summer. Nobody remembered that Laura and Gertrude were left alone.

Gertrude was curled up asleep on the floor. Laura sat on the perch in her cage, watching Gertrude with beady eyes.

"Gertrude!" Laura called presently. "Kitty!"

Gertrude opened one eye. Then she opened the other eye. She rose slowly. Suddenly she sprang toward the parrot's cage.

Laura began to squawk and beat her wings, but there was nobody to settle the fight.

When Mrs. Einstein came in from the garden, she found Laura's cage lying on the floor. "Albert!" she cried. "Albert, come quickly! Something has happened to Laura!"

Albert rushed downstairs. His heart almost stopped when he saw the open door of the cage and the green feathers scattered about.

Laura was nowhere in sight, but Gertrude lay on the hearth, sleeping peacefully. Her fat black sides puffed slowly up and down as she breathed. Albert didn't want to believe his eyes.

It was an unhappy family that sat down to dinner that night. Everyone admitted that Laura was a problem, but the family loved her just the same. Maja cried so hard she couldn't eat. Albert didn't try to comfort her. It was all he himself could do to keep back the tears.

After supper Albert said he wanted to be alone. He didn't feel like talking. Sadly he climbed the stairs to his room.

"Albert!" cried a weak little voice. "Albert!"

Albert jumped and looked up with disbelief. It couldn't be, it just couldn't be! Nevertheless, there was Laura, perched on the head of Albert's bed. She looked like a half-plucked chicken. "Mother! Father!" Albert cried happily. "Uncle Jacob! Maja! Here's Laura!"

The children's tears were dried in a hurry. While the family was talking things over there was a knock at the door. It was the neighbor and her friend. When the friend saw Gertrude, she agreed that Gertrude was her cat. Nobody, not even Maja, cared to argue about that.

"Cats and parrots don't mix," said Mr. Einstein later, "but I know something that will."

"What's that?"

"A puppy!"

"Why, of course," said Mrs. Einstein. "Laura can call a dog as much as she likes. A dog can't reach her cage, and Laura can't get to the dog."

The next day Mr. Einstein brought home the prettiest little puppy in all of Germany.

Maja named him Gerald. He and Laura became very good friends.

A NEW FRIEND

ONE AFTERNOON IN late summer Albert went for a walk along the Isar River in Munich. He liked to walk. He liked to look at the earth and the sky. He liked to look at trees and flowers, butterflies and birds. Sometimes there were so many things to look at that he wandered far from home.

It was a beautiful afternoon, sunny and clear, with a cool wind coming down from the mountains. Albert strolled along contentedly, enjoying the fresh air and the beautiful countryside.

Presently he saw a young stork lying in the

grass near the path. As he drew closer, the stork fluttered its wings and tried to hop away. Then Albert saw that it could not stand on its legs. One leg seemed to be broken.

"Oh, the poor thing!" he thought. "I wish I could help it."

He left the path and started across the grass. The frightened bird struggled harder than ever. It was headed straight for the river as fast as two wings and one good leg could carry it.

Albert caught up with the bird at the edge of the river. He reached down to pick it up. At that moment his foot slipped and he fell into the water with the stork under his arm.

Albert gasped. The water was cold because it had come from the mountains. The stork beat at his face with its wings, but he held on. Half wading and half swimming, he made his way back to the bank.

The bank was steep and covered with grass. With his feet and his one free hand, Albert scrambled upward. There wasn't a root or a bush to hang on to, and he slid back. He tried again and again. Each time, he slid back into the water, while the stork struggled to get away.

Albert could have climbed out easily enough if it hadn't been for the stork. However, he was determined to save the stork and he wouldn't give up. After resting for a few moments in the icy water, he tried again.

"Hold on!" somebody shouted suddenly. "I'll help you!"

Albert looked up. A fair-haired young man was running across the grass toward the river. He picked his way down the bank and held out his hand.

"Here!" he cried. "Take hold of my hand!"

Albert seized the outstretched hand and the young man quickly pulled him out of the water and up the bank to dry land.

Albert dropped to the grass, panting for breath. "Thanks!" he gasped. "I was trying to help this stork and fell in the river. Look! The stork has a broken leg."

"It's a good thing I saw you," said the young man. "That water must be awfully cold. My name is Max Talmey. I'm a medical student at the University here."

Albert scrambled to his feet, still holding the stork. "I'm glad to know you," he said, shaking the other's hand. "I'm Albert Einstein."

"Are you Hermann Einstein's son?"

"Why, yes," replied Albert in surprise. "Do you know my father?"

"I've met him," said Max. "My brother introduced me to your father just a few days ago.

Your father invited me to come to your home for dinner tonight."

"Then you must have been on your way now. I'll take you there," Albert said.

Suddenly Max Talmey burst out laughing. "If you aren't a sight!"

Albert looked down at himself and laughed, too. He was covered with mud from head to foot, and he couldn't tell whether the stork under his arm was white or mud-colored. All at once his teeth began to chatter.

Max Talmey stopped laughing. "We'd better get you home in a hurry," he said. He took off his coat and put it around Albert's shoulders. Then he took the stork. "Come on, Albert," he said. "Show me where you live. After you're taken care of, I'll have a look at the stork. Maybe I can set his leg."

Albert led Max home by the shortest road. All the way they were busy talking. By the time they reached the house, each of them had told the other all about himself.

Max said he was twenty-one years old. He didn't have much money, but he was determined to be a doctor. He had come to Munich to study at the University.

Albert said he was ten and a half. He had finished primary school. Now he attended the Luitpold Gymnasium in Munich. The teachers didn't like him because he asked so many questions. Sometimes they thrashed him when he asked. He would like to forget about school.

"I'm certainly glad you came along today," Albert said. "It was lucky for the stork, too. Not every stork is cared for by a real doctor."

"Well, I'm not quite a doctor yet," Max said with a twinkle in his eye. "Let's hope the stork won't find out."

"It won't!" Albert laughed. "I'll never tell."

Then they reached home. Albert presented his new friend to his mother and told her about his adventure with the stork.

A GUEST FOR SUPPER

Albert wanted to begin work on the stork's leg right away, but Mrs. Einstein wouldn't hear of it. First she made Albert change his wet clothes. In the meantime she made some hot tea. Then she gave Albert and Max each a big piece of fresh coffee cake.

After Albert was warm and dry, he and Max and Mrs. Einstein turned to the stork. Mrs. Einstein found some pieces of light wood for splints. She tore an old sheet into strips for bandages. She helped make a nest for the stork in the Einstein carriage house.

Albert held the patient while Max worked. In a short time the stork's broken leg was set.

"Now, Albert," said Max, pretending he was a real doctor, "I think our patient is resting comfortably. I'll turn it over to you."

Albert's eyes shone with merriment. Max was more fun than anybody he knew, except Uncle Jacob. "Yes, Doctor. What shall I do now?"

"The most important thing is to see that the

patient has a steady diet," Max said, still serious. "Do you know what storks like to eat?"

"Fish, frogs, and insects, I think."

"Also eels, toads, mice, and other small animals," Max added.

"It looks as if I'm going to be busy chasing stork food," Albert said with a frown.

"Yes, indeed!" Max grinned. "Come on, I'll help you catch the patient's first meal."

"Max, when you and Albert return, I'll have supper ready," Mrs. Einstein said.

"Yes, ma'am!" Max smacked his lips. "After that coffee cake, I can hardly wait."

Albert was delighted with his new friend. So were the rest of the Einsteins. Maja called in her dog, Gerald. She wanted Gerald to walk on his hind legs for Max.

Albert showed his parrot to Max. He taught Laura to call Max by name.

At the supper table Mrs. Einstein filled up the guest's plate again and again. Later when he had left, she spoke to her husband. "Hermann, we must invite Max to come often. Why, that boy's so thin! I don't think he has enough to eat."

"Now, Pauline," Mr. Einstein said with a smile. "You're always worrying about people. I think you're wonderful for it! Of course we'll ask Max to come again."

"Besides," Mrs. Einstein added, "I'll always be grateful to Max. Why, Albert could have drowned today. We might never have seen him again if it hadn't been for Max."

"Indeed he could!" said Uncle Jacob seriously. "We owe Max a great deal."

"Max doesn't have much money, but he's determined to be a doctor," Albert said, hoping to change the subject.

Mr. Einstein tousled Albert's hair. "You're quite taken with Max, aren't you?"

"Max is smart," Albert replied. "He can answer all kinds of questions. I can learn a lot from him, Father."

"He's a deserving young fellow," Uncle Jacob agreed. "He will find it hard and costly to become a doctor, but we'll certainly find a number of ways to help him."

"If Max can answer Albert's questions, he'll be a help to us, too!" Mr. Einstein said with a hearty laugh.

"I WISH I KNEW THE THINGS YOU KNOW"

Every Thursday night after that the Einsteins invited Max for supper. Each week Max checked his patient, the stork. After four weeks he removed the splints from the stork's long red leg. It looked exactly like the other leg, but there was no way to tell whether it had healed enough for the bird to fly.

"Well, there's one way to find out," said Max. "Let's set the stork free."

"Maybe it won't want to fly away," Maja said. "I hope not."

"Oh, Maja!" groaned Albert. "I hope it *can* fly. You should try to feed a stork sometime!"

"Poor Albert!" Mrs. Einstein laughed. "He's hardly had time for his own food. He's been so busy finding food for the stork."

"Look!" Albert cried happily. "There it goes!"

The stork had sprung into the air and was flying higher and higher, with its long legs sticking straight out behind. It was a beautiful sight. At last the stork came down again and circled around as if to say, "Thank you, my friends, and good-bye!"

"You're going to be a fine doctor, Max," said

Mrs. Einstein. "Your first patient certainly did all right."

"Thank you," said Max, as pleased as he could be. "I had good help."

"I'm worried," Albert said. "How will the stork find its way to Africa? It's almost winter. All the other storks have left."

"It won't get lost," Max replied. "Young storks always have to find their way alone. Something inside them guides them all the length of Africa to their winter nesting grounds."

"There's an old stork's nest on our roof," said Maja. "Maybe the stork will come back to us next year."

"I hope you're right, Maja," said Mrs. Einstein. "We always want a stork family on our roof. It brings good luck."

"Well, I want the Einsteins to have all the good luck possible," said Max, "but that nest belongs to another stork family. They'll probably return next year to claim it. They'd be unhappy if this stork moved in."

The Einsteins laughed.

"Of course they would!" Albert said, looking at Max admiringly. "I wish I knew all the things you know, Max."

"Why, thank you, Albert," Max said. "For a boy of ten and a half I'd say you know quite a bit already."

"He does," said Mrs. Einstein proudly. "Albert's going to be a fine professor someday."

"Why, I've just the thing to help him learn more!" Max exclaimed suddenly. "Why didn't I think of it before?"

"What?" cried Albert.

"Books! A whole set of them! They're called *Popular Books on Natural Science.*"

"Books!" exclaimed Mrs. Einstein. "There's nothing Albert likes better."

"Oh, Max, you won't forget to bring them next Thursday night?" Albert cried.

"Next Thursday night," Max promised. "I won't forget, Albert."

After that Albert could hardly wait from one Thursday night to the next. He read the books again and again. Then he and Max talked about the things he had read.

They talked about animals. They talked about plants. They talked about stars, meteors, volcanoes, earthquakes, and climate.

"Don't you two ever run out of something to talk about?" teased Uncle Jacob one night.

"Never!" declared Albert.

Mrs. Einstein laughed. "I declare, I don't think they ever will."

THE BOOMERANG

IT WAS A RAINY night in April 1890. Albert met his friend Max at the door when Max came for supper. "Come in, Max, come in!" Albert cried.

Max shook the rain from his hat before stepping inside. Then he looked at Albert closely. "What's going on? You sound excited."

"I am," said Albert. "Tonight I have a surprise for you, Max."

"A surprise? For me? Where? What?"

Albert grinned. "I'll tell you in a minute, Max. First let me hang up your hat and coat."

Just then Uncle Jacob came into the living room and greeted Max. He was followed by the rest of the family, for they all liked the young medical student.

"Albert's been working on this surprise for days," Mrs. Einstein whispered.

"He wants to thank you for the books you've brought him," Mr. Einstein added.

Max looked puzzled. "I can't imagine what the surprise is."

"I know," Maja giggled. "It's a—"

"Shh," warned her mother. "Here comes Albert. Let Albert tell about the surprise."

Albert was glad there was nobody present but his family. Even then he was so shy he could hardly say a word. He carried a paper in his hand. He handed it to Max. "This is for you, Max," Albert said, his face growing red.

Max took the paper. He read it slowly while

all the Einsteins watched. Max grinned as he read what Albert had written.

"Read it aloud," shouted Uncle Jacob.

"Yes, read it to us, Max," cried Maja, making herself comfortable.

"Of course I'll read it," Max said, getting to his feet slowly. He cleared his throat and rattled the paper once or twice. Then, in a clear loud voice, he began to recite.

"Listen, folks, for here are the facts.
I have a friend by the name of Max.
His hands are quick, his eyes are keen.
To be a doctor is his dream.

"And when his goal is reached, by jing!
He'll be the best, a very king,
The best from here to old New York.
For proof just ask a certain stork.

"Then broken bones should cause no worry,
For Max will fix them in a hurry.
And if you have a pain, don't fret or yell.
Ask Max—he'll come and make you well.

"But doctoring is only part
Of Max's knowledge; he's so smart
That he can tell about a snail
Or just as well discuss a whale.

"He's learned the causes for a storm
And why a hive of bees will swarm.
The distance to the moon he knows,
And what makes color in the rose.

"Yet the best thing about my friend
Is his willingness to lend
His books to make me smarter, too.
So thanks, friend Max, my thanks to you."

The listeners shouted with laughter. Max laughed, too. He liked a good joke, even about his doctoring.

"I didn't know we had a poet in the family," teased Uncle Jacob.

"Albert writes songs, too," said Maja. "I often hear him singing them."

"This is the first time I've had a poem written to me," Max said. "I'm very proud."

"We may laugh at Albert's verses," said Mrs. Einstein, "but Albert meant every word of them, Max. You're his dearest friend."

Such talk as this made Albert blush. He didn't like to be the center of attention. Nevertheless, he was pleased that Max and the family had liked his poem.

Max dug deep in the pocket of his coat. "That reminds me, Albert. Here's another book I've been telling you about."

"What a funny title for a book," Maja said,

peering over her brother's shoulder. *"Force and Matter!* What does that mean?"

"I can explain that, Maja," Albert said. "Anything that occupies space and has weight is called matter."

"Am I matter?" Maja asked, giggling.

"You are indeed," said Uncle Jacob. "Everything about us is matter, even air. Even though you can't see it, air has weight."

"Now that you've explained matter, tell us about force," Mrs. Einstein said with a laugh.

"There are many different kinds of force," Max said. "To begin with—"

"I know one of them," Albert interrupted. "It's the force that makes the magnet and the compass work."

"Another is the force called gravity," said Uncle Jacob. "Gravity is the force that pulls matter toward the earth."

Albert's eyes shone. "Oh, I've read about gravity," he cried. "It's the force that makes water run downhill. It's also the force that pulls air toward the earth. That's why balloons go up. They weigh less than air. As air is pulled toward the earth, it crowds the balloons up, away from the earth."

Uncle Jacob laughed. "Well, I see you've finally solved the puzzle of the balloons at the *Oktoberfest*."

"What new puzzle are you working on now, Albert?" asked Mr. Einstein.

Albert never had a chance to answer, for Maja interrupted. "What's that noise?"

"Noise!" Mrs. Einstein moved toward the window. "It sounds like a parade of wagons going by the house."

Parade was right! Albert peered through the rain. He saw elephants, zebras, and camels plodding behind a long string of wagons.

Albert threw open the door so that the family could see better. "It's the circus coming into town," he cried.

"Why, of course," exclaimed Uncle Jacob. "I saw a circus poster just the other day. Now how would you and Maja like to go to the circus tomorrow, Albert?"

"We'd love it!" cried Albert and Maja.

THE AUSTRALIAN BUSHMAN

Albert enjoyed everything he saw at the circus the next afternoon, but he surprised his Uncle Jacob. Uncle Jacob thought he would prefer the lions and tigers or the elephants, or perhaps the clowns or bareback riders. Albert enjoyed all of those, and the monkeys and trapeze performers, too. Most of all, however, he enjoyed the Australian bushman.

This Australian bushman, or native, was a fierce-looking creature whose black skin shone with war paint. All he wore was a loincloth, but in his hands he had several curved sticks.

The bushman stood at the side of the circus ring, looking savage. The ringmaster cracked his whip and shouted, "Presenting the one and only Jo-Jo and his boomerangs!"

"What's a boomerang?" Albert whispered.

"It's a kind of hunting weapon," Uncle Jacob

explained. "It's used by the Australian natives. They throw the boomerang so it will strike their prey. If it misses, it comes back to them."

Up stepped Jo-Jo with his boomerangs. Suddenly he hurled one of the curved sticks. It flew straight toward the crowd.

Women shrieked, and even men ducked their heads in alarm.

"My goodness, somebody's going to get hurt!" cried Albert.

Just before the boomerang reached the crowd, it shot up into the air. It made a big circle and sailed right back to Jo-Jo's hand. The audience cheered and clapped.

Again and again Jo-Jo threw his boomerangs. Sometimes one would hit the ground and bounce into the air again. Sometimes it would make one circle in the air before it returned, and sometimes two or even more. At other times it would sail as high as the top of the circus tent, but it always came back to Jo-Jo.

Albert, Maja, and Uncle Jacob could hardly believe their eyes.

"It doesn't seem possible, does it?" said Uncle Jacob.

Albert said, "I'm going to figure out how he does it. There must be an explanation."

"Here we go again," Uncle Jacob said with a smile. "Albert's found another puzzle."

ALBERT MAKES A BOOMERANG

Albert soon discovered that making a boomerang was not easy. He talked the problem over with Max. He talked with Uncle Jacob. He talked with his father. He read everything about boomerangs that he could find in books. Nobody could help him much. Boomerangs were used mostly in Australia, and there were no Australian bushmen in Munich to give him advice.

A boomerang looked just like a long curved stick. However, Albert soon learned that it was a great deal more. It had to be carved from green, hard wood. The inside edge had to be sharp and the outer edge slightly rounded. Then the ends had to be warped or twisted just right so that the boomerang would fly back properly when thrown.

Making a boomerang might have been easy for Australian bushmen, who had been taught how to do so by their fathers. It was not easy for a little German boy. He had to be pretty clever to figure it all out.

Albert worked for a week before he was ready to try his boomerang. It rose in the air, but it did not return to him as Jo-Jo's boomerang had. Albert started all over. The next boomerang was better. It came back about three times out of five.

One evening Mr. Einstein watched Albert as he warped the ends of a boomerang over a fire.

"What are you going to use the boomerang for?" he asked. "Are you going hunting?"

Albert looked shocked. "No, never!" he cried. "I'll never hunt! I couldn't kill anything!"

"Then your boomerang isn't a very useful thing, is it?" asked his father. "Don't you think you'd better study your Latin and Greek?"

Albert shook his head. "I've learned a great deal about mathematics working on this boomerang," he said.

"Perhaps you have learned something, but the teacher says you're doing very badly in school," replied his father. "Except in mathematics, of course. I'm sorry, Albert, but you must put your boomerang away. Only when you have finished your homework can you get the boomerang out."

Albert obeyed his father, for in his heart he knew that his father was right. If he had worked just a little harder on something besides mathematics, he could have made better grades at school. From now on he would really try. He wouldn't even take time to play with Maja.

One evening Maja took Gerald out to the garden to play. For a while she threw a stick for him to return to her.

At last her mother called, "It's getting dark, Maja. You and Gerald had better come in."

"Please, Mother, may I stay out just five minutes longer?" Maja begged.

"Oh, all right," Mrs. Einstein agreed. "I suppose nothing could happen to you out there."

Something did happen, though. A big bat

swooped out of the sky and flew straight at Maja. Maja screamed. Gerald barked and did his best to protect her. Mr. Einstein ran to the garden followed by Mrs. Einstein, Uncle Jacob, and Albert. They were all alarmed.

"A bat!" cried Uncle Jacob.

"Are you hurt?" cried Mr. Einstein.

"I don't think so," Maja sobbed. "It just frightened me. I'm afraid of bats, Father."

"I know, my dear. Many people are. I doubt whether it would hurt you, though."

"I wonder if that bat is living around here," said Uncle Jacob.

"I don't know," replied Mr. Einstein. "I'd like to chase it away somehow, if it is. I don't want it frightening the children."

"How can we chase a bat away?" Uncle Jacob asked. "We could kill it."

Mr. Einstein shook his head. "I don't want

to kill it. Bats help get rid of insects. If I could only knock it down or catch it somehow—"

Albert tugged at his father's coat sleeve. "Father, why not try my boomerang?"

Mr. Einstein looked down at him thoughtfully. "That's not a bad idea," he said. "Maybe we could use your boomerang. You'll have to show us how to use it, though."

Albert showed his father and Uncle Jacob everything he had learned. Soon they could throw the boomerang as well as he could. The next evening they waited in the garden for the bat.

Suddenly the bat was there above them, fluttering and flickering in and out among the shadows. It flew straight at them and was gone before they could even move.

"I'll be ready for him the next time!" Mr. Einstein said.

A moment later the bat came back. Mr. Einstein's arm moved quickly. The boomerang flew through the air, and the bat fell to the ground with a shrill little cry.

Mr. Einstein, Uncle Jacob, and Albert hurried forward.

"Is it dead?" asked Albert, a little sadly.

Uncle Jacob bent down carefully. "I don't think so. I think it's just stunned. If you'll get me a box, Albert, I'll take the bat away. I'll set it free some place where it won't bother us again."

"Albert, this boomerang is all right," Mr. Einstein said later. "I guess it was a good thing you made it after all."

"Then you're not angry with me now, Father?" Albert asked.

"Of course not, son," Mr. Einstein said gently. "Just the same, you must give more attention to some of your other subjects in school. They are just as important as mathematics, even if you don't like them as well."

"I'll try, Father," Albert said. "I really will. You just wait and see."

GEOMETRY AND VIOLIN CONCERTS

ONE MORNING IN 1891 Albert came downstairs to breakfast. Uncle Jacob took one look at him and looked at Mr. Einstein. Mr. Einstein looked at Uncle Jacob.

"Something strange is going on," said Uncle Jacob. He was puzzled.

"Very strange," Mr. Einstein agreed.

Albert's hair was combed. His shoes were polished. He was neatly dressed, and his mother had not said a word to him.

He sat down at the table and ate his breakfast

quickly. Then he went into the next room to feed his parrot, Laura.

"There's nothing wrong," said Mrs. Einstein. "Don't you remember? This is the first day of school. Albert's ready to go."

"He was never this eager to go to school before," said Mr. Einstein, shaking his head.

"There's a reason this year," Mrs. Einstein answered, smiling. "Albert begins to study geometry. He's looking forward to it. He told me so the other day."

"No, Pauline! It can't be!" Mr. Einstein burst out laughing. "Why, you know Albert. He's as balky as a mule about going to school. I know geometry is one of the most interesting and useful kinds of mathematics. I know Albert's eager to learn it, too, but—like school?"

"Just the same," said Mrs. Einstein, "it's true."

It *was* true, too. Albert had been looking

forward to geometry for a long time, and he was actually glad that school was starting. He even hoped that he would begin to like school.

He never had, of course. German schools were strict. The teachers barked out orders like army sergeants, and the boys had to jump to attention. From morning to night they had to drill, drill, drill, like soldiers. They never could think for themselves.

Albert's mother had tried to explain to him why German schools were like an army. The army was very powerful in Germany, she said, and many people admired it. These people thought that schools should be run just as the army was run. After all, every German boy had to become a soldier when he grew up. He might as well start learning to be a soldier while he was still in school.

Albert was still not convinced. This morning,

however, he said to himself, "Oh, well, no matter how school turns out this year, there's going to be one bright spot."

"Bright spot!" said Laura.

"Yes, Laura," Albert laughed. "Bright spot! My geometry class!"

THE GEOMETRY GAME

The first day of school was over, and Albert was in his room. He was getting ready to prepare the next day's lessons. "Which shall I do first, Latin, Greek, history, geography, or geometry?" he thought. He smiled and without hesitating opened the new geometry book.

Once he began to read he forgot about his other studies. He forgot about school. He even forgot what time it was. Suddenly he heard his name called. Somebody was shaking his shoulder. He looked up. It was Uncle Jacob.

"Wake up, boy!"

"Oh! Uncle Jacob!" Albert cried. "I wasn't asleep. Look! I was studying my new geometry book! It's wonderful!"

Uncle Jacob laughed. "I might have known. Didn't you hear? Your mother has been calling you for fifteen minutes."

"Why, no!" Albert looked at his uncle in astonishment. "I'm sorry. I didn't hear a thing."

"I believe you," said Uncle Jacob, closing the geometry book with a snap. "Come along now, before supper gets cold."

At the table, Albert told the family about his geometry class.

"You couldn't study anything more useful," said Uncle Jacob. "Geometry teaches you how to measure and compare lines, angles, surfaces, and solid objects. Just about everything around us has to do with geometry in some way."

"Really?"

"I'll give you an example," said Uncle Jacob. "Look at your knees and your elbows. Think of all the angles they can form. Those angles are part of the study of geometry."

"Why, of course!" said the astonished boy, bending his arm. "I can make all kinds of angles. I never thought of that before."

"The branches of a tree make angles, too," added Mrs. Einstein.

"A wheel is a circle," said Maja.

"The earth is a ball or sphere," said Mr. Einstein quickly.

"So is a marble," cried Albert.

"This tablecloth is a square," said Uncle Jacob. "You see, we find geometry all around us, no matter where we look."

"This is just like a game!" Maja said. "Let's play the geometry game again sometime."

By the end of a week Albert had worked almost all the problems in the geometry book by himself. That didn't mean that he would stop thinking about geometry, however. Neither would the rest of the Einsteins. They all enjoyed the geometry game and played it every night. Each tried to outdo the others. They were all amazed that nature used geometry in so many different ways.

"Bees know geometry," said Mr. Einstein, walking into the house one evening with a package. "Here's some honey to prove it."

"Why, Hermann, you're right!" exclaimed Mrs. Einstein. "Come, everybody, look! See the six-sided pattern of the honeycomb."

"A six-sided figure is a hexagon," said Mr. Einstein, pleased with himself.

"Geometry or not," added Uncle Jacob, "honey is good eating."

All the Einsteins laughed.

"Today I learned that spiders know geometry," said Maja proudly. "I watched one. I counted eight sides to the web it spun."

"Eight sides," said Albert. "I learned the other day that an eight-sided figure is an octagon."

Now it was Mrs. Einstein's turn. "Well, today I had a geometry lesson from a fish," she said seriously.

"A fish!" The others roared with laughter.

"Laugh if you like," she said. "I've cleaned many a fish, and I know. Their scales overlap in a regular pattern."

"They do. That's a fact, Pauline. That's a very good thought," said Mr. Einstein.

"My lesson in geometry is a big one," Uncle Jacob spoke up. "It's a volcano."

"Now, Jacob, how could a volcano use geometry?" asked Mrs. Einstein.

"A volcano forms a cone when it erupts."

Everyone had to agree that he was right.

"I've been thinking about a soap bubble," said Albert, "and how it forms a sphere."

"Splendid, Albert," said Uncle Jacob.

"How lucky I am!" thought Albert that night when he was alone in his room. "I don't have much fun at school, but I certainly have fun at home. Still, how could I do otherwise with a wonderful family like mine?"

FUN FOR THE EINSTEINS

Playing the geometry game wasn't the only way the Einsteins had fun together. There were other ways, too. They went to concerts and puppet shows. They went for outings in the mountains. They went sailing on nearby lakes.

Cold wintry evenings they spent around the

fireside at home. Then Mr. Einstein read to the family from his favorite German poets, and Mrs. Einstein played to them on the piano.

Albert often accompanied his mother now.

"This is supposed to be fairy music," she would tell him. "Let's try to make it light and airy now."

Or maybe it was a gypsy dance they were playing. Then she would say, "You should play this with spirit, Albert."

Albert wanted to please his mother and put his whole heart into playing just right.

"Why, Albert!" his mother exclaimed one night. "You're doing better every day!"

Albert was beginning to enjoy the violin now. He played it more and more. By the time he was fourteen he played very well.

One day when he was in his room getting his homework, Maja knocked on the door.

"Albert," she said, "Mother wants you to come downstairs for a moment."

"Why?" he asked. "What's wrong?"

"I don't know. There's a strange man talking with Mother in the parlor. They're talking about you and your violin."

"My goodness, why?" said Albert. "I'll come at once. I wonder what he wants."

Albert and Maja hurried downstairs to the front hall. Albert smoothed his hair and straightened his coat. Then he entered the parlor.

"Mr. Gerhart, this is my son, Albert," said Mrs. Einstein. "Albert, Mr. Gerhart is the leader of a small orchestra here in Munich. He has paid you a great honor."

Albert bowed. "I don't understand, Mother."

"Of course not," said Mr. Gerhart. "Let me explain. Our little orchestra is giving a concert next week. It's for the benefit of the orphans in

Munich. Now, at the very last moment, one of our violin players has become ill."

Albert looked puzzled.

Then Mrs. Einstein spoke. "Mr. Gerhart is wondering whether you would like to play in the sick man's place."

"Oh, Mother," said Albert, "I don't play well enough for that."

"Nonsense," said Mr. Gerhart. "I've been told you play very well."

"Albert does play well," Mrs. Einstein said, smiling proudly, "but he has never played in public. I'll leave it up to Albert. I want him to decide if he would like to try."

Mr. Gerhart spread a piece of music out on the piano. "Here's one of the things we will play," he went on. "Would you care to play it for me, Albert?"

"I'll try," said Albert, picking up his violin.

"Good work, Albert," said Mrs. Einstein when he had finished.

"Splendid," said Mr. Gerhart. "You read music very well. Now, Albert, what do you say? Will you help us out at the concert?"

"I'd like to help the orphans," said Albert. "Yes, if you think I can, I'll do it."

Mr. Gerhart was delighted. He gave Albert the music the orchestra would play at the concert. He told Albert about the rehearsals.

After Mr. Gerhart left, Mrs. Einstein beamed with pride. The rest of the Einstein family was just as proud. All they talked about now was Albert's concert.

Mrs. Einstein told all her friends. They all said they would buy tickets.

Maja told her schoolmates. Mr. Einstein told his customers.

One evening Uncle Jacob said that he had walked past the concert hall. He almost burst with pride, he said. There on a big poster in front of the hall was "A. Einstein, violinist."

Albert didn't feel proud. The closer the day of the concert came, the more he wished that he had never heard of it.

"You're having stage fright," said Uncle Jacob. "You'll get over it."

At last the night of the concert arrived. Albert's mother wore a new blue dress, and Maja wore a new red one. Mr. Einstein and Uncle Jacob wore their best suits, and so did Albert.

Best suit or no best suit, however, Albert was frightened. His hands were shaking. He wondered if he would even be able to pick up his violin, let alone play it.

"Just look at that crowd of people," said Uncle Jacob proudly when the family reached the concert hall.

"Yes, just look at them," thought Albert. "I'd better run away while I still can."

It was too late to run away now, however. The lights were being dimmed. People were finding their seats. In two minutes the curtain would go up, and he, Albert Einstein, would be on the stage in front of all those people.

Worst of all, he was the only boy in the group. The other three members were men, and all of them were fine musicians.

Out in the audience Mr. Einstein whispered to his wife. "I hope Albert is over his stage fright. Maybe we shouldn't have let him play."

"You wait," said Mrs. Einstein. "Albert will forget his stage fright before he has played six notes. He'll be thinking so hard about the music he won't know anybody's here."

"That's right," agreed Uncle Jacob. "You know as well as I do how lost Albert sometimes becomes in thought."

That was exactly what happened, too. For one awful moment Albert shook with fright. Then he heard Mr. Gerhart tap his violin bow for the music to begin.

Albert lifted his bow and began to think about the music. Here it was like a fairy skipping at play. There it was heavy and sorrowful. Again it was wild and fiery. Soon Albert was so busy that he forgot all about the crowd.

Before he knew it the concert was over.

Then each member of the group came to the front of the stage to take his bow.

When Albert stepped forward, there was a roar of applause. "Bravo!" the crowd cried.

Albert's face grew red, and he didn't know where to turn. He wished that he could sink through the floor, but he couldn't.

Afterwards Mrs. Einstein gave him a big hug. "Albert, you were the hit of the show."

"I enjoyed it," said Albert. "All except taking those bows."

"Well, you'd better get used to that," said Uncle Jacob. "Someday you might be famous."

"No." Albert shook his head. "Not me!"

"Don't be too sure," teased his uncle.

GOOD-BYE, GERMANY!

FOR A LONG TIME business at the Einsteins' electrical shop had been growing worse. Meanwhile business for another shop nearby had been growing better.

The owner of the other shop was the brother of an important general in the army. Many of the Einsteins' customers took their business to the other shop. They said they couldn't help it. They were afraid to do otherwise. They didn't want to get in trouble with the army.

In 1894 Hermann and Jacob Einstein had

to close their shop. There was nothing else for them to do, for they had no business left. They were not giving up, however. They began to look around for a new place to start business. Relatives in Milan, Italy, wrote that they thought Milan might be just the place.

"My goodness," said Maja, "won't it be exciting to live in Italy?"

"I'm sorry about your business, Father," said Albert, "but I'm glad to leave Germany. Now I won't have to become a soldier."

"Hold on there," said Mr. Einstein. "Not so fast, Albert. I thought you planned to go to a university someday."

"Yes, Father, I hope to."

"Then I'm afraid you'll have to stay in Germany for a while. You'll have to finish school. You can't enter a university without a diploma from the gymnasium."

"Hermann, I believe you're right," agreed Mrs. Einstein. "I never thought of that."

"Where will I live?" asked Albert.

"We'll find a place for you to board," said his Uncle Jacob. "You can join us in Milan as soon as you finish school."

Immediately Mrs. Einstein began to worry. "Albert has always been so close to all of us," she said. "Perhaps we shouldn't leave him here in Munich alone."

"Now, Mother, I'm not a baby," Albert said. "What Uncle Jacob says is true. I can come to Milan later. I have only one more year at the gymnasium and then I'll be finished."

Finally everything was settled. Albert had a place to live, and the family was ready to leave. Albert went to the railroad station with them to say good-bye. His heart was heavy, but he tried to be brave.

"I'll see you all in Milan a year from now," he said, as cheerfully as he could.

Maja could hardly keep from crying. "I'll send you a letter from Italy every day," she promised. "I'll tell you all about it. Maybe you won't feel so far away from us then."

"Take good care of yourself, son," advised Mr. Einstein. "Work hard. The year will go faster if you keep busy."

"Don't go walking in the rain without your coat," warned Mrs. Einstein.

Albert had to grin at that. He knew how his mother always worried about him. Still, she *was* right. He often went for a walk in the rain, and it never occurred to him to put on his coat. He would be thinking so hard that he wouldn't even notice the weather.

"Keep up the good work with your mathematics," Uncle Jacob said, "but give Latin and Greek some attention, too. Maybe you can finish school in less than a year."

Now the train began to move. Albert ran beside it for a little way.

"Good-bye, Albert," the family cried, waving from the window. "Good-bye!"

"Be sure to write to us every week," called his mother.

"I will." Albert waved sadly. "Good-bye!"

He stood on the station platform, waving until the train was out of sight. For the first time in all his fifteen years he was completely alone. He couldn't even turn to his friend Max Talmey for comfort, for Max, too, had left Munich. He had finished his medical studies and had gone to America to be a doctor.

ALONE IN MUNICH

The Einsteins had arranged for Albert to stay in the home of Mr. and Mrs. Weissmann. Mrs. Weissmann was a friend of Albert's mother. She and her husband did their best to make Albert feel at home.

So did the Weissmann children, Sarah, Leonard, and Solomon. They enjoyed having Albert live at their house. They had always wanted a big brother.

Wherever Albert was, Leonard and Solomon were right on his trail. Sarah was almost as bad. The children never left Albert at peace for a moment. They were after him from the time he got up until he went to bed.

The first thing they did each morning was run to Albert's room. "We're already up, sleepy-head," they would tease.

Of course, they didn't have to tell Albert they were up. He knew it. He had heard them coming. Now he might as well get up, too. He would have no rest until he did.

Mrs. Weissmann knew that Albert had to be left alone when he was getting his lessons. She told the children never to bother him when he was trying to study.

Sometimes the children forgot. Solomon, the youngest, would peep around the door of Albert's room. If Albert was at his desk, then in Solomon would come. He would climb right up in Albert's lap. "Albert, tell me a story."

Albert didn't have the heart to say no. He

would drop his studies and begin a story for the child.

Sarah quickly learned just where to turn when she needed help with her arithmetic. She went straight to Albert's room. Albert would know the answers, she knew. He always did.

Albert couldn't even play his violin in peace any more. Leonard had a drum. At the first note from the violin Leonard would come running with his drum.

"Pretty music," he would say.

Albert didn't think it was pretty. He couldn't bear the clatter of the drum, and he got his violin out less and less.

Of course, the children meant no harm, and Albert knew it. Just the same, he missed the quiet of his old home. He missed his mother's cooking. He missed the pleasant evening meals.

He missed the family discussions about algebra, geometry, music, electricity, and all the things they used to talk about.

TROUBLE AT SCHOOL

At school Albert was still an outsider. He didn't fit in. He never had. He knew now that he never would.

He was not good at sports, but athletics were part of the school course. Good or bad, every boy had to take part in them.

One day the boys were choosing up sides for a game of tug-of-war.

"We'll never win if we have Einstein on our team," one captain said.

"We don't want him, either," said the other captain. "He's too solemn and slow."

"I guess you heard the question he asked in class the other day," said the first captain.

"What is light made of?" mocked the second. "Yes, I heard it."

"The teacher got so red in the face I thought he was going to burst."

"Of course. He didn't know the answer."

"Well, who does?"

"Who cares?"

"Einstein cares, I suppose."

"Well, then, let Einstein figure it out for himself," the second boy declared.

Albert was standing not far away. He didn't hear everything the boys were saying, but he could guess the rest easily enough. The same thing had happened before, with these and other boys. It hurt to be unwanted. He wished that he could be like other boys, but he didn't even know how to try.

A month dragged by, then two—then three, four, and five. Maja kept her promise. There was seldom a day that she missed writing to him. Instead of helping, however, her letters made him feet worse. Italy was the liveliest, happiest place on earth, she wrote. The family missed him very much.

Well, Albert missed them, too! He didn't care if he never got a diploma from the gymnasium. At last he made up his mind. He was going to Italy as soon as he could find a way.

Albert thought about the problem for a long time. Maybe he could say that he was sick. That really wouldn't be untrue. He had been studying hard. He was tired and so lonely that he could almost die.

Yes, he decided finally, that was what he would do. He would ask old Dr. Stern to help. Dr. Stern had been a friend of the Einstein family ever since Albert was a small boy.

Dr. Stern listened carefully to Albert's story. Then he listened to Albert's heart and to his

lungs. He checked Albert's pulse. He looked at Albert's tongue.

At last he sat back in his chair and looked at Albert. "Albert, you *do* need a rest," he said. "I'll write out a request for you. I'll say that you should leave Germany and go to a better climate for a while."

Then the doctor put his hand on Albert's shoulder. He looked into Albert's eyes and smiled. "Don't worry about being different from other boys. Just keep on using that good mind of yours. Keep on asking questions, too. Someday you'll find the answers. Someday those other boys will wish they were like you."

Albert's heart was light as a feather after that. He didn't feel lonely. He didn't feel tired. He felt wonderful. The only thing that hurt was his conscience. Could he honestly turn in that request from Dr. Stern? Did he really need a rest from school?

Before he had a chance to decide what to do, the decision was made for him. His science teacher told him to stay after class one day.

"Einstein," he said, "do you know what a bad influence you are on the other students in this class? They don't respect me as their teacher because I can't answer your questions."

"I don't mean to cause you trouble, sir."

"Well, you do cause trouble," grumbled the teacher. "Take a look at some of the questions you've asked." The teacher pulled out a notebook. He flipped over some pages and read. "'Why can't we feel the earth move?' 'What is space?' 'What keeps the world from flying into pieces as it spins around?'"

The teacher took a deep breath. He was growing angrier by the minute. "Einstein, I can't answer those questions. Neither can anybody else. There are no answers. Don't you understand? No answers at all!"

"I'm sorry, sir."

The teacher hadn't finished yet. "What's more, I've been talking to some of your other teachers. We all agree. We think you should withdraw from the gymnasium."

"Oh!" Albert was shocked. "Am I being expelled from school?"

"No, Einstein. You've broken no rules. We can't expel you for asking questions. We'd just be glad to see you leave. We think you'd be happy to leave, too."

"I certainly would," thought Albert, "and that's just what I'll do. I won't have to use Dr. Stern's request after all."

Before he left the school, Albert prepared for the future. He had a long talk with his mathematics teacher.

"Yes, Einstein," nodded the teacher. "You are far ahead of the other students in mathematics. In fact, you're far ahead of many university students. As far as mathematics is concerned, you're ready to enter a university now."

The teacher sat down at his desk. He wrote rapidly for a few moments. Then he handed Albert the paper on which he had been writing. "Here, Einstein. Here's a statement. Maybe this will help you get into a university without a diploma from the gymnasium."

"Thank you, sir. I'm grateful to you."

Albert turned and walked away. He could hardly believe it. All he had to do now was to get on a train for Italy. There was a train leaving in just a few hours, but he would have to hurry to catch it.

Sarah, Leonard, and Solomon sat on the edge of Albert's bed and watched Albert pack. Their eyes were as big as saucers. For once they could think of nothing to say.

"I've grown fond of you little rascals," Albert said, smiling.

"They'll miss you," said Mrs. Weissmann, who came into the room just then. "So will I." She handed Albert a brown paper package. "Here's some lunch and supper. We don't want you to get hungry on the train."

"Why, thank you!" Albert said.

He shut his bag with a snap. He picked up the bag, the brown paper package, and his violin case. That was all he owned in the world.

"Good-bye!" called the Weissmanns.

"Good-bye!" called Albert.

Then Albert hurried to the railroad station. He was just in time, for the train was ready to leave. He was out of breath when he found his seat, but he wasn't too tired to enjoy himself.

He laid back his head. He heard the shrill toot of the whistle. He listened to the chug, chug of the locomotive. Faster and faster the train went on its way to Italy.

"It's really true," Albert thought. "I'm saying good-bye at last. Good-bye, Germany!"

WONDERFUL ITALY

ALBERT WAS HAPPY to be in Italy. He was happy to see his family again. In fact, he had never been so happy.

The family was happy to see Albert, too. They didn't even scold him for having been put out of school in Munich.

"You're fifteen now," Mr. Einstein said. "It's time you began to decide things for yourself. Of course, you will make mistakes at times. Everybody does. Then you must learn to take the consequences of your mistakes."

"Thank you, Father," Albert said. "I understand. If I made a mistake, I won't complain."

Albert loved Italy. It was completely different from Germany. There was no goose-stepping army to order people about. The Italian people thought, studied, and worked exactly as they chose. They were free.

After he had been in Italy a while, Albert decided that he no longer wanted to be considered a German. He told his father this.

"Very well," Mr. Einstein agreed. "I know how you feel about Germany. If you wish, you may give up your German citizenship."

"I know I'll have to start back to school somewhere soon, Father," Albert went on. "Before I do, I'd like to visit Genoa."

Mr. Einstein shook his head. "I wish I could say yes to that, too, Albert, but I'm afraid I can't. Genoa is a long way from

Milan, and I have no money to spare for such a trip."

"It won't cost much," said Albert. "I have it all worked out. I'll walk."

"Walk!" cried Maja. "Why, you'll have to cross mountains, Albert!"

"Where will you sleep?" asked his mother.

"Under the stars," Albert replied. "Italy is a beautiful country, and I'd like to see more of it while I can."

"I agree," said Uncle Jacob. "Why, if I had the time, I'd do the same thing myself."

"All right," agreed Mr. and Mrs. Einstein.

Off Albert went, headed for Genoa, with a knapsack on his back. He had only enough money to buy food for the trip. He had a few books to read and a change of clothes, and that was all.

He traveled slowly. He didn't want to miss anything along the way. He stopped to look at sheep grazing on the hillsides. He paused to watch villagers in the town squares.

He admired the vineyards planted like steps on the slopes of the hills. He smiled at the farmers pressing the grapes in huge barrels. When they hopped from the barrels, he laughed aloud. Their bare legs were stained purple to the knees from stomping out the juice.

Albert could not speak or understand Italian

very well, so he could not talk with people much. There was one thing he could understand, however, and that was music.

There was music everywhere in Italy. The smallest goatherd played the pipes as he watched his flock. Even when Albert went to sleep on a lonely hillside at night, he could hear music. It might be accordion music from a festival in the village or voices singing as they prepared for bed, but there was music.

Once Albert awoke suddenly in the middle of the night. There was no music now, but he could hear something moving. Whatever it was, it was nearby. Albert's heart almost stopped.

"Can it be a wolf?" he wondered. His father had said there were wolves in the mountains.

"Maybe it's a bandit!" Albert thought. Mrs. Einstein had worried about bandits. She said robbers were on every path.

"Well," Albert decided, "I can't lie here in the dark forever. I'll have to find out."

As quietly as a mouse, he crept in the direction of the sound. Then suddenly he stopped and burst out laughing. The sound had not come from a wolf or even from a robber. It had come from a donkey no bigger than a dog.

Albert laughed with relief. "Poor little fellow! He must be lost. In the morning I'll have to see if I can find his owner."

Albert tied the donkey to a bush. Then he lay down again, with his head on his knapsack. He was not sleepy now, so he lay for a while looking up at the stars.

Suddenly he jumped up. The sky was full of falling stars. He had seen one falling star before, but this was a whole shower of falling stars. For a few moments the sky looked like a big fireworks display.

"Little donkey, how glad I am you came along!" Albert said after the stars had disappeared. "Otherwise I'd have slept right through that wonderful sight."

Albert thought about the stars for a long time. He knew that falling stars are not really stars but small pieces of iron or stone that enter the earth's atmosphere. As they speed through the air they grow white-hot and are easily seen from the earth. They burn up quickly and few ever reach the earth.

"Where do the stone and iron come from to begin with?" Albert wondered. "What's out there in that space beyond the earth? Ever since Father gave me the compass years ago, I've been wondering about these things."

Then Albert made another decision. "When I return to school, I'm going to study physics. Physics is the study of heat, light, sound, magnetism,

electricity, and many other things. Perhaps through physics I can learn the answers to some of my questions," he thought.

SCHOOL AGAIN!

When Albert returned to Milan a month later, bad news awaited him. The Einstein electrical shop had never done well in Milan. Mr. Einstein had decided to close up shop again and move to Pavia, Italy.

"Albert," he said, "your vacation must end. It's time for you to decide what kind of work you want to do."

"Maybe you would like to become an electrical engineer," suggested Uncle Jacob. "You've always been interested in electricity. We could use your help in the shop."

Albert shook his head.

"I know a business career is out," Mr. Einstein

said sadly. "Albert has never been interested in business."

"Would you like to be a professor?" asked Mrs. Einstein hopefully.

Albert smiled. His mother had always wanted him to be a professor. "I might become a professor of mathematics," he said. "I'd like to study physics, too."

"Forget physics, Albert," said Mr. Einstein.

"Remember, you don't have a diploma from the gymnasium," Uncle Jacob warned. "A university may not accept you as a student. You may not be able to study physics."

"I've thought about that," Albert answered. "There's a school in Zurich, Switzerland, called the Swiss Federal Institute of Technology. If I showed the statement from the gymnasium about my work in mathematics, I might be accepted there."

"Very well, then, we'll try to see you through," said Mr. Einstein.

"We want you to have an education," Uncle Jacob said, nodding his head in agreement. "We'll help all we can."

"It won't be much, though, because business has been bad," added Mr. Einstein.

"I understand," said Albert. "I won't ask for much. I'll leave for Switzerland at once."

SWISS AT HEART

ONE BRIGHT MARCH morning in 1895, Albert arrived in Zurich, Switzerland. He was sad at having left his family again, but he was eager to finish school. Now if only he could persuade the Swiss Federal Institute of Technology to let him enroll in its classes!

As soon as he got off the train, Albert asked the way to the school. Then he brushed his suit and combed his hair. He bought a cinnamon cake for his breakfast. He ate the cake as he walked toward the school.

For the hundredth time Albert checked his pocket to make sure the statement from his mathematics teacher at the gymnasium was still there. That piece of paper was to be his way of entering the new school. Whatever happened, he didn't want to lose it.

When he finally reached the school, Albert suddenly felt very young. Students hurried in every direction. They all seemed quite grown up. Albert had just turned sixteen a few days before, and he felt out of place.

In the office Albert waited his turn to see the Director. At last the Director called his name.

"Come in," he said, smiling. He was a kindly, white-haired man. He asked Albert to sit down while he read the letter.

Albert looked at the floor. He looked at the ceiling. He looked at the books on the shelves. He looked out the window. From time to time he stole a look at the Director. What was the Director thinking? Was he ever going to speak?

At last the Director raised his head. He peered at Albert over his glasses. "Splendid, Einstein! You have a splendid record in mathematics."

Albert's heart soared. Then it fell just as quickly as the Director added, "Of course, there are other subjects besides mathematics."

How often Albert had heard that story before!

"Then I won't be permitted to enter the school?" he asked.

"On the contrary, Einstein. Because of your record in mathematics, I'm going to give you a chance. On one condition!"

"What is that?" asked Albert eagerly.

"Since you have no diploma, you'll have to take the entrance tests. If you can pass the tests, then I'll say no more. You'll be a full-fledged student of our school."

"Thank you, sir," said Albert. "Thank you very much. I'll do my best."

A week later Albert was back at the Director's office, along with several other young men. For one reason or another they had all taken the tests. Now they were waiting to hear how they had done. One by one they were called into the Director's office. One by one they came out, some with happy faces, some with sad faces.

At last Albert's turn came. He rose to his feet. His hands shook. He dropped his hat. He almost stumbled as he made his way into the Director's office.

The Director pointed to a chair. Albert sat down. Then the Director began to talk.

"I'm sorry to have to tell you, Einstein, but your tests show that we cannot accept you as a student in this school."

"I—I failed?" Albert's voice was trembling.

The Director nodded. "You gave a good account of yourself in physics and mathematics. In everything else the results were bad."

"I'm sorry, sir," said Albert sadly. He rose to leave. "Thank you for your kindness."

"Wait," called the Director. "May I suggest that you go back to a gymnasium and get your diploma? Then come back. We'd like to have a student with your ability in mathematics."

"Thank you, sir." Albert tried to smile, but his heart was heavy. Go back to the gymnasium? Go back to a school like the one he had left in Munich? Just as well sentence him to prison!

"There's a good school in Aarau about thirty-five miles from Zurich," suggested the Director. "Why don't you go there?"

"I—I'll think about it, sir."

The Director had been more than kind.

Albert knew that. He knew something else, too. Six months ago he had left the gymnasium in Munich without waiting to get his diploma. Now the results of that bad decision had ruined his chances of getting into the Institute. It was like a boomerang that had come back to him.

Albert was deep in thought as he left the Director's office. He was in a bad spot, but he was not going to give up so easily. If the only way he could get into the school at Zurich was by a diploma, he would return to a gymnasium. He would go to Aarau. He would go there and get a diploma just as fast as he could.

ALBERT FINDS HE LIKES SCHOOL

Before he had been in Aarau a week Albert had the surprise of his life. The school here was so different from the one in Munich that he actually liked it. Not only that, he liked Switzerland and the friendly Swiss people.

One day after school a classmate came up to Albert. His name was Karl Winteler. His father was one of Albert's professors.

"Come home with me tonight," Karl said. "Have supper with us. My Father and Mother would be happy to have you."

"I—I'd like to," Albert said shyly, "but I need to study."

"You don't have to study all the time. Father says you're one of his best students."

"Me? The best student?" Albert laughed.

"What's so funny?" asked the puzzled Karl.

"I'm sorry, but in Munich the teachers always said I was the worst in the class." Albert hesitated. "I believe I will come home with you after all. I guess I won't study tonight."

"Good," said Karl. "Let's go."

Albert liked the Wintelers at once. They were friendly and kind and treated him as one of the family.

After supper everybody sat by the fireplace and talked and roasted chestnuts.

Albert enjoyed himself very much. At last Mrs. Winteler turned to her husband. "Bring out your accordion," she said. "Play some good music for us."

"I wish I had my violin with me," said Albert. "I'd join you."

"Bring your violin tomorrow night," said the Professor. "We'll play a duet."

"I have a better idea," said Mrs. Winteler. "Why doesn't Albert come and live with us while he's going to school? Then he'll always have his violin handy for a duet."

"That's an excellent idea!" cried Professor Winteler. "Einstein, what about it?"

"Yes, Albert, please come," said Karl. "Just think of the pleasant times we could have."

"There's a small room in our attic. It isn't very large, but I think you'll find it comfortable," said Mrs. Winteler. "We promise not to bother you when you want to study."

Albert was so pleased that he hardly knew what to say. How good the Wintelers were! How would he ever be able to repay them? Of course he would come!

PLANS FOR THE FUTURE

Time passed quickly for Albert now. He was happy in school. He was permitted to ask as many questions as he wished.

He was happy with the Wintelers, too. They were wonderful friends who never gave him a chance to be homesick.

The year went by so fast that before Albert

knew it spring had come again. One day in June Mrs. Winteler said, "Why don't you boys go for a walk and pick some wild strawberries? I'd like to have a strawberry tart."

"I would, too," said Karl. "How about it, Albert? Would you like to go?"

"I'm willing," Albert said.

Away the boys went, up the river and along the edge of the forest to the southern slopes where wild strawberries grew. Each boy carried a small basket, but the baskets filled slowly. The boys ate more berries than they saved.

At last Albert stopped picking. "I don't have to be a mathematician to know we'll never get a strawberry tart this way." He laughed.

"You're right," Karl said. "Let's just pick berries from now on."

"We can still talk. In fact, if we aren't eating, we can talk all the more," Albert said.

"I feel sad today," Karl said presently.

"Sad!" exclaimed Albert. "Why?"

"This is probably the last time we'll go tramping through the woods together. You'll finish school in a few weeks. Then I suppose you'll go away somewhere."

"Well, yes, but I'm only going to Zurich," Albert said. "The Swiss Federal Institute of Technology can't turn me down now."

"Where will you go after you finish school in Zurich? Back to Italy?"

"No, Karl. I believe I've always been a Swiss at heart," Albert said. "The Swiss people love freedom. So do I. I'm going to stay in Switzerland. I've decided to become a citizen of Switzerland when I'm twenty-one."

"Hooray!" shouted Karl. "This calls for a real celebration! Let's hurry home!"

"A strawberry tart celebration," Albert added.

The two friends hurried home with their baskets of strawberries. It was nearly time for supper. If there was going to be a strawberry tart, they had to move fast.

PROFESSOR EINSTEIN

BY 1907 ALBERT EINSTEIN had been a citizen of Switzerland for several years. What is more, he had a job working for the Swiss government in Bern. He liked his new country, and he liked his job as a patent examiner.

Whenever an inventor in Switzerland had a new invention, he would send it to the government in Bern to be examined. If it was found that the invention had not been thought of before, the inventor could have a patent on it. That meant that no one else had a right to use the inventor's idea or to copy it.

Of course, patent examiners had to be very alert to tell whether or not an invention was new. There was not a better examiner anywhere than Albert Einstein.

"I've never seen an examiner like Einstein," said the Director of the Patent Office one day. "He does in three hours the work that another man needs all day to do."

"Yes, but what does Einstein do with the rest of his time?" asked another examiner scornfully. "He just sits and dreams."

"Or writes foolish papers which nobody understands, like those he wrote two years ago," said another examiner.

"I must agree with you there," said the Director sadly. "I like the man, but I can't understand his ideas. I doubt whether anyone else can understand them, either."

Many people would have laughed scornfully had they heard what the director said. These people not only understood Albert Einstein's ideas but were quite excited about them. They were the world's scientists.

Ever since 1887 scientists had been trying to solve a big puzzle. For hundreds of years they had believed that the sun was like a ball hanging in space. They believed that the sun remained always in the same spot and the earth and other planets moved around it. As for the space that wasn't occupied by the sun, the other stars, and the planets, the scientists believed it was filled with something they called "ether."

No one had ever proved these beliefs. However, they seemed reasonable, so scientists thought they were true.

Then in 1887 two scientists conducted an experiment. This experiment seemed to prove either that the earth did not move through space or that there was no such thing as ether.

Some scientists wanted to give up one belief. Some wanted to give up the other.

Albert Einstein became interested in the problem and began to think about it. In 1905 he wrote several papers in which he gave his ideas on the problem. These ideas were so new and different that scientists everywhere took notice.

Professor Kleiner of the Physics Department

at the University of Zurich was one of these scientists. One day he went to Bern to talk with Albert Einstein.

He half expected to find a cocksure young fellow too proud even to speak with an old professor. He was quite surprised when he met the dark-haired young man with warm brown eyes.

Albert held out his hand in greeting. "It's an honor and privilege to meet you, Professor Kleiner," he said.

"The honor is mine," Professor Kleiner replied. "I'm proud to talk with a young man who has given science so many new ideas."

"You are too kind, sir."

"Too kind!" exclaimed the professor. "You are too modest, Einstein. I know a new idea when I see one. First, you say that space is not filled with ether. Instead, you say, space is nothing at all. Then you say that the sun is not fixed in space."

"Indeed not!" said Albert. "I believe the sun is moving constantly. So are the other stars and planets. The whole Milky Way and every other galaxy like it are hurtling through space."

"Of course, every schoolboy who has ever studied geometry knows the three dimensions, length, width, and thickness," Professor Kleiner went on. "However, you've added a new one, Einstein. You say that time also is a dimension."

"Ah, yes." Albert nodded vigorously. "It seems to me the only way the universe can be described accurately and scientifically is with the three dimensions of space and the one of time. You can no more separate them than you can separate the width of a box from its height."

Professor Kleiner smiled. "Your ideas about motion are new, too, and yet quite obviously true. I don't know why I didn't think of them myself. We could never tell we were moving unless there was another object by which to judge our movement."

Now it was Albert's turn to smile. "I see you have read my papers."

"Yes, I have, and I found them very interesting," the professor said. "I was especially interested in the paper on light. You think nothing moves faster than light."

"That's true," Albert replied. "Light is the fastest thing in our universe. Not only that, the speed at which it travels is the only thing in our universe that never changes. It is always the same, everywhere.

"Light isn't what we think it is at all. We think of it as an endless, continuous thing, a steady flow like water, but it isn't. I tried to prove in my paper that light is made of tiny particles of energy, which I call photons."

"You know, Einstein, all these ideas are

quite new to the world of physics," Professor Kleiner went on. "It will take scientists a while to understand them and to determine whether or not they are true."

"They are true," said Albert quietly. "I'm sure of that. I think I can prove all of them."

"I'm sure you can," replied the professor, smiling. "Someday when you have time I wish you would prove one for me. In one paper you said that mass and energy are the same thing, and that one can be changed into the other. To me that idea is the hardest to understand."

Albert laughed. "Someday, if our paths cross again, I shall prove it for you," he said.

"Ah!" Professor Kleiner slapped his forehead. "That reminds me! Einstein, you should not be working in a patent office. You should be a teacher in a university."

"No, no!" Albert shook his head. "I like my

work at the Patent Office. Besides, I tried to find work as a teacher once. After I graduated from the Institute at Zurich, I wanted to teach, but nobody would hire me. I nearly starved until I got this job at the Patent Office."

"Well, we'd be proud to have you teach at the University of Zurich," said Professor Kleiner. "That is why I came to Bern—to offer you a job at the University. Of course, there is one thing you must do to qualify."

"What is that?" asked Albert politely.

"You must give private lectures first. In that way you will prove to the University that you can teach, and you will gain experience at teaching at the same time."

"Thank you," Albert said thoughtfully. "Perhaps I will." He smiled. "My mother always believed I would be a professor someday. She has said so ever since I was a little boy."

ALBERT BECOMES A PROFESSOR

At last Albert Einstein was a professor. His mother's predictions had come true. He had taught at the University of Zurich. Now he was in Austria as a professor of physics at the University of Prague.

This did not mean that Albert had stopped working on his own problems. On the contrary, he thought about them every minute that he wasn't teaching. He wrote more papers, too.

One day in 1912 Albert's friend, Professor Pick, stopped in Albert's office at the University. He wanted to congratulate Albert on his latest paper, in which Albert had said that light bends as it travels through space. This idea was just as new and different as his other ideas. For centuries scientists had believed that light always traveled in a straight line.

"The wonderful thing about this idea," said

Professor Pick, "is that you've shown scientists how to prove it."

"It can be proved the next time there is a total eclipse of the sun," Albert said. "Of course, most of the time the light of the sun makes it impossible for us to see the light from the stars near the sun. I believe that if we could see that light we could determine that it actually bends as it passes the sun.

"The only trouble is that we'll have to wait a while for our proof. Eclipses of the sun don't happen every day."

"When the next eclipse happens, I'm sure that we'll find you are right," Professor Pick said.

"It's good to talk with a friend like you," said Albert. "You remind me of another friend I had when I was a boy in Munich. His name was Max Talmey. What splendid times we had discussing science!"

"Was he a scientist?"

"He was really a medical student, but he was deeply interested in science. As a matter of fact, it was he and my Uncle Jacob who first aroused my interest in science."

"Well, I hope I'm here when this idea of yours is proved correct." Professor Pick rose and took up his hat. "You'll be a famous man then, Einstein. I want to be the first to congratulate you if I may."

"Thank you, Pick, but I'm afraid we won't be together when the next eclipse occurs," Albert replied. "I am returning to Zurich shortly. I have been asked to become a professor at my old school, the Swiss Federal Institute of Technology, and I have accepted. I like Switzerland and shall be happy to return."

WORLD FAME

Professor Pick was right. In 1919 the whole world was talking about Albert Einstein.

There had been a total eclipse of the sun that year. Two groups of scientists had traveled to Brazil and Africa, where the eclipse could be seen. They had taken pictures not only of the sun but of the light from the stars near the sun. The pictures showed what Einstein said they would. As the light from the stars passed near the sun, it bent almost exactly as much as he had said it would.

After this, people everywhere began to think more seriously about Albert Einstein's ideas. Few people really could understand them. However, if one of his ideas had been found to be true, it seemed likely that the rest were true. Almost everyone began to think so.

By this time Albert lived in Berlin, Germany. He was a professor at the University of Berlin, one of the best universities in Europe. He did not spend all his time in Berlin, for other universities wanted him to talk to their students, too. He traveled to England and the United States. He traveled to China, Japan, and Palestine. He traveled all over Europe.

Wherever he went, people liked him. They did not always understand what he said, but of one thing they were certain. Albert Einstein was one of the world's most intelligent men. He had given it many new things to think about.

When Einstein came to visit the United States, a great crowd gathered at the harbor to welcome him. There were parades and banquets. Everyone wanted to meet him.

In China the teachers and pupils of the German School came down to the pier to greet him. They sang to him in German.

In Japan the day of his arrival was made a national holiday. He was received by the Empress of Japan herself.

Of course, the people of Germany were very proud that Albert Einstein had been born in Germany. They gave him many gifts to show how proud they were. One of the gifts that he enjoyed most was a sailboat. It was given to him by the people of Berlin because of the honor he had brought to their city.

There was one German who didn't like Albert Einstein, however. His name was Adolf Hitler. Adolf Hitler was a political leader. At first he had no power to harm Einstein or anyone else, but as the years passed his power increased. At last he became the sole ruler of Germany, with power of life and death over the people.

Hitler didn't like Jewish people. He especially didn't like a Jew as famous and intelligent as Albert Einstein. He did everything he could to make Einstein's life difficult.

Finally Albert decided to leave Germany.

"I cannot fight a tyrant like Hitler and do my work, too," he said. "I can work anywhere, so why should I stay in Germany? I shall accept that offer to work at the Institute for Advanced Study in Princeton, New Jersey."

ALBERT EINSTEIN, AMERICAN

IT WAS CHRISTMAS EVE of 1933. In the little town of Princeton, New Jersey, a group of young men and women was going from house to house, singing Christmas carols. Their music echoed through the frosty winter air and made all who heard it feel better.

At last the carolers approached an old-fashioned cottage on a quiet side street.

"This is Professor Einstein's home," said one young woman as she pulled her coat more tightly about her against the winter air.

"Can you imagine being driven from your country just because you're a Jew?" said a tall young man as he shook the snow from his hat. "What a terrible experience that must be!"

"The German government under Hitler seized Einstein's home and all his money," said another. "Einstein realized that he wouldn't be safe anywhere in Europe. That was one reason why he came to this country."

"It seems to me Hitler has caused nothing but trouble in the world," someone said.

"He has brought sorrow to a great many people, and not only to the Jews in Germany," the leader replied.

By this time the carolers had gathered in a group in front of the Einsteins' house. For a moment they watched the house in silence, each thinking his own thoughts.

At last the tall young man said, "It seems to me

Hitler's rather foolish. When he drove Einstein out of the country, Germany didn't gain a thing. It was the United States that gained. We ought to be proud that Dr. Einstein chose to live in Princeton."

"I'll go even farther than that," said the leader of the group. "I think I'd be speaking for the whole country when I say we ought to be proud that Einstein has chosen to live in the United States." He raised his hands. "Now, let's begin. Let's sing 'Silent Night.' That's a German carol that Einstein will be sure to know."

Once more the voices rang out. After "Silent Night," they sang "Joy to the World" and "Hark! the Herald Angels Sing."

After the last song, the carolers paused for a moment. Suddenly they were surprised to hear a violin echoing the song which they had just finished. Through the darkness they made out a shadowy figure standing on the porch.

"Why, it's Dr. Einstein!" one of the singers gasped. "He's playing our carols!"

"Good evening!" It was Einstein speaking. "I want to thank you all for the music. It was beautiful." He opened the front door. "Won't you all come in and warm yourselves for a while? We can have more music and talk."

The carolers accepted the invitation proudly. They felt honored to be invited into Albert Einstein's home.

Later, as they were leaving, one young woman said, "You know, Einstein looks just like his pictures. I'd have known him anywhere with that flowing white hair and those big eyes."

"The thing that surprised me was that he was so shy," another caroler said. "I don't know what I expected, but I didn't expect such a famous man to be so quiet and—and humble!"

"Well, he doesn't try to impress people," said

the tall young man. "He doesn't want to. He thinks only of his work."

"He's friendly, though," added another. "He has spoken to me many times on the street."

The group walked down the snow-covered walk in silence for a moment. In almost every house they saw a brightly lighted Christmas tree, a symbol of the peace and goodwill for which Christmas stands.

Presently someone said, "I'm glad we stopped to sing at the Einsteins' home. I think our carols meant something there—perhaps more than at most places. We were being friendly to a person who for a long time had found little or no friendship in his own country. Maybe our singing will help to make the Einsteins feel at home here."

The leader nodded thoughtfully. "Yes, I think he and Mrs. Einstein appreciated our carols."

"I hope he stays in Princeton," said the wife of the tall young man. "I like him."

"He will," the leader replied. "Didn't you hear him say that he hopes to become a citizen of the United States someday?"

A GREAT AMERICAN

One spring day in 1954 Billy and Frances Fleetwood came home from school very late. Billy and Frances lived in Princeton, New Jersey.

"My goodness, where have you two been?" their mother exclaimed.

"We stopped at Mr. Einstein's house on Mercer Street," said Billy. "He's been helping us with our arithmetic."

"Dr. Albert Einstein?" Mrs. Fleetwood exclaimed in astonishment.

"Yes, I think that's his name," Billy answered. "He's old and has long white hair."

"He's the nicest man, Mother!" Frances said. "He makes arithmetic seem just as easy as—as playing hopscotch. He explains it better than the teacher does at school."

Mr. Fleetwood laughed. "No wonder! He's one of the greatest mathematicians in the world."

"Oh, dear!" Mrs. Fleetwood looked worried. "I hope you children haven't been bothering him. He's a very busy man."

"I don't think so, Mother," Billy replied. "He said to stop whenever we wanted help with our arithmetic lessons."

"That sounds like him," Mr. Fleetwood said with a smile. "He likes children."

Just then the children's Aunt Mary entered the room. "Who's this you've been visiting—Albert Einstein?" she said.

"Yes, Aunt Mary."

"How did you become acquainted with him?"
Aunt Mary asked curiously.

"Do you remember the day you gave me my
bicycle?" Billy asked.

"Of course!" Aunt Mary said. "You must have
fallen off a hundred times that day!"

Billy smiled. "Well, that's how I met Dr. Einstein. That afternoon I tried to ride up the Mercer Street hill."

"He fell off," Frances interrupted, "just as Mr. Einstein came along."

"Mr. Einstein helped me get on the bike again and then showed me how to ride."

"Then we got to talking about other things," Frances said. "I told him how hard arithmetic was for me, and he said he knew how I felt. He said when he was a boy in Germany he used to have trouble getting his lessons. I told him I couldn't understand fractions, and he promised to help me. He did, too."

"Well!" Mr. Fleetwood was amazed. "I hope you two understand what a rare privilege you've had. You've become friends with one of the greatest men in the world."

"A great American, too," Aunt Mary added.

"He's an American citizen now, you know. Even before he became a citizen, though, he was worried about the safety of our country, which he had come to love. In 1939 he wrote a letter to President Roosevelt. In this letter he warned the President that the Germans were working on an atom bomb. He also reminded the President of an old idea of his. He said that this idea could lead our scientists to the actual design of an atom bomb.

"Do you know what happened?" she went on. "Before those scientists started to work, they had to study one of the papers which Albert Einstein had written back in 1905!"

"When the first atom bomb was dropped on Japan in 1945, it proved that Einstein's idea was right," Mr. Fleetwood added. "It didn't make Einstein happy. In fact, he was sad, because he had always wanted his work used to make the world a better place to live."

Billy looked thoughtful. "I know that's true! He's such a—such a kind man. I'll bet he wouldn't hurt a fly if he could help it."

"Fortunately, most of the things that have come from Dr. Einstein's ideas have been useful and worthwhile," Mr. Fleetwood said. "I'll bet you children didn't know that every time you watch television you owe it to Dr. Einstein."

"Television!" cried Frances.

"Yes, indeed. Dr. Einstein found the explanation of what scientists call the photoelectric effect in 1905. As a result of this discovery, scientists since then have developed television cameras, sound movies, and the electric eye."

"What is an electric eye?" Billy asked.

"It's a device used to count people, open doors, operate burglar alarms, and do many other wonderful things," his father explained.

"Dr. Einstein was given the Nobel Prize for

his discovery of the photoelectric law," Aunt Mary put in.

"You've been talking only about Dr. Einstein's work in science," Mrs. Fleetwood said. "What about the other things he has done? I remember reading not so long ago that he had been offered the presidency of the country of Israel."

"Yes, that's true," said Mr. Fleetwood. "It was a great honor, too, offered because he had done so much for Jewish people throughout the world. He was the second person to be chosen for that position."

"He turned the honor down, though," Mrs. Fleetwood said. "He said that he was a scientist and had not been trained to serve as president of a country."

"It seems to me that shows what a modest man he is," Aunt Mary said thoughtfully. "In spite of his great work and all the honors that he has received, he thought he was not qualified to be a president How many men would feel that way, I wonder?"

There was a moment of silence, during which Billy and Frances thought about what they had heard. Finally Billy sighed.

"You know, I never thought too much about Mr. Einstein before," he said. "Now that you've told me about him, I'm mighty proud to know him. He must be a great man."

"So am I," Frances said, giggling. "Just think! Someday I can tell people that Albert Einstein helped me with my arithmetic!"

THE FOURTEEN GREATEST SCIENTISTS

One day Mr. and Mrs. Fleetwood took Billy and Frances to New York City. One of the many places they visited was Riverside Church, overlooking the Hudson River.

As they approached the church, the children

saw many figures carved in stone above the doorway. They looked at the figures curiously.

"Who are those people?" Billy asked.

"The one in the center, above the door, is Christ," said Mr. Fleetwood. "Those in the five arches surrounding him are angels and the world's greatest scientists, philosophers, and religious leaders. Look at the figures in the second arch from the outside."

Billy and Frances studied the figures overhead. Suddenly Frances uttered a cry of amazement.

"Why—why, there's Mr. Einstein!" She turned to her father in bewilderment. "It *is* Mr. Einstein, isn't it, Father?"

"Yes, it is," said Mr. Fleetwood. "The fourteen men in that arch were chosen as the greatest scientists in the history of the world. The men in the arch below it are the world's greatest philosophers, and those in the arch below that

are the greatest religious leaders. Of all those men, Albert Einstein was the only one who was chosen when he was still alive."

"Just think what an honor it was," Mrs. Fleetwood put in, "to be included here with the greatest men in the world."

"These men were chosen by scientists, philosophers, and religious leaders all over the country," Mr. Fleetwood said. "I think it was an even greater honor that Einstein was the only scientist, living or dead, whose name appeared on every list."

"Why were all these people put up here?" Billy wanted to know. "What are they all supposed to mean?"

"This doorway is supposed to show that Christ is just as much concerned with the world today as when He was on earth. Since His time, however, the world has changed, and the changes were brought about by the men who are shown here on these arches."

For a few moments Billy looked thoughtfully at the figures overhead. Then he said, "I knew Mr. Einstein was smart, but I didn't know he was such an important man!"

"He's a very remarkable man," Mr. Fleetwood

said. "I think probably the greatest thing about him is the fact that he has refused to accept an idea as true unless it was proved to be true.

"When he was a little boy he asked questions about everything. He continued to ask questions when he was a man. He didn't give up when he was told that no one could answer those questions. He just went to work and found the answers himself. His search led to a whole new way of looking at the universe in which we live. Even though few people really understand his ideas, his work has brought about tremendous changes in our ways of thinking and living."

There was another short silence as Billy and Frances looked up at Einstein's figure. Then Billy said in an awed voice. "Golly, Frances, we've been learning arithmetic from a real mathematician!"